SONG FOR SIMONE

And Other Stories

by Jacob Ross

Karia Press

Song For Simone
and other stories

First published in 1986 by **Karia Press.**
Copyright © Jacob Ross, 1986.
Front Cover Illustration from photograph by Carl Gabriel
Back Cover photograph by Lance Watson
Cover Design by Buzz Johnson
Typeset by Karia.

ISBN 0 946918 29 5 Pb
ISBN 0 946918 33 3 Hb

Karia Press,
BCM Karia,
London,
WC1N 3XX.
United Kingdom.

Made and printed in Great Britain by the
Guernsey Press Co. Ltd., Guernsey, Channel Islands.

Contents

For Doods
For Lexia
For Grenada

Author's Note

The author wishes to thank all those who have contributed, directly or unconsciously, to the creation of this collection.

I thank in particular, the following:

Maria Wilkinson, my mother, for the quality of her courage. **Jacqueline Creft** for pointing me forward. **G. Payne B.** For pointing me inward. **Samuel Philip,** my father, for his gift of words and images. **Chris Searle** for his encouragement.

Finally, a word of thanks to **Merle Collins** for her invaluable, detailed advice and support. And to **Buzz Johnson** for his expressions of confidence.

Without them, this book might still be a wish, briefly entertained, never pursued.

Publisher's Note

In this book, Jacob Ross brings to our attention some of the real experiences of children and youth and show the communities as they are. Set in Grenada, the stories ring of issues which are tied-up with the pressures we face there and the struggle to break-out and move into a new situation. These are universal realities and have relevance to the lives of people from other parts of the world. Thus, the reality of oppression and the persistence of struggle exist wherever poverty prevails, and it is with a focus on struggle and change that lessons can be learnt from experiences.

The eventual publication of this collection is the result of a co-operation between the author (and his associates) and Karia Press (and its friends). It is Karia's first full publication of 'prose' and marks the beginning of our titles for younger people. These are also of great relevance to other readers. We hope the stories will be instructive for all readers. For us, learning is the *key* word because it is only by engaging in the process of sharing information that ideas change and develop.

A Game of Marbles

Ken wakes. Marbles are on his mind. Last night he dreamt of new ones. They were sitting in a ring staring up at him, like eyes of shining glass, each with its own foliated iris of burning purple, red, green, white or blue. He has also dreamt of birds — big, fat ones, strutting inquisitively round the ring of marbles. They had hard, round, shiny eyes of steel.

Ken blinks the sleep away. His eyes are like marbles too — big tors — peering sadly into the morning, above the wall of hills.

In the road below, a Land Rover snarls past. All through the night, they have been bolting up and down the road and he wonders, for the millionth time, if the soldiers ever slept; if they ever found time to put down their guns, ignore the curfew and pitch marbles in the road.

Dada, the old woman, wouldn't have slept one wink! She will talk all day about the shots she'd heard, the Rovers tearing through the dark, keeping her frightened and awake. She will speak of all those nameless, terrifying things that she is too old to understand. And she will later ask him, when the strike will end and people be able to walk the road again to find food, and friends?

Ken never knows what to tell her; so, he shrugs, shakes his head and says nothing because he is not sure he understands either. It is marbles that he understands. Playing makes him forget food and Dada's feebleness.

There are no more wild yams where he sometimes go deep into the bushes to search them out. Dada knows it is not only he who hunts the hills for yams· and that the plot of land behind the house holds no more food. It has already surrendered every root and leaf.

She tells him to eat; forgetting about herself, knowing that he's sick of the green bananas she boils, steams, stews, fries or roasts for him each day.

The greeness of the land around no longer holds the promise of abundant food. So, Ken pitches marbles with his friends and tries to forget his grandma's ailing; not from age, as she has said, but because bananas and wild yams are not enough. She needs meat.

He too craves meat; his small body begs for it. Any meat would do, even saltfish; but the shops are closed, their doors padlocked and chained from everyone. Everything has stopped.

He made a new slingshot the day before. Went into the bushes to find the small Y-shaped branch, stripped it, pared it down to size and shaped the handle to his liking. He then covered it with the strips of rubber that he had razored from a car's used tube. At each tip of the forked stick, he tied firmly down, two special straps of red rubber of equal lengths obtained this time, from a truck's tube. Finally, to the ends of the powerful rubber-straps, he joined a single leather-tongue taken from an old shoe. The straps became a single loop; the tongue, the place where he would place the stones to shoot.

After, Ken went into the forest to search for birds. He spared the *cee-cee* birds. They were too small, and not good for eating either! His craving had pushed him to the upper reaches of Mount Airy. There, he sent a *Pikayo* careering earthward in a cloud of grey and white feathers. But it was not the same bird that had stood a moment before, perched on the branches of the tall silk-cotton tree, whistling its soul away. On the carpet of rotting leaves, it seemed no more than a flaccid heap of feathers still warm with the life of its unfinished song.

Ken felt like crying — he was so sorry. He buried it beneath the same tree with a muttered apology and a prayer.

He felt little guilt, however, for the mountain dove he

shot an hour later. It was a plump, pigeon-like bird; soft feathered and golden brown. Very tasty too!

The boy couldn't help wondering, though, whether the dove had young ones, a husband — he thought it was a lady — and a home. Did they ever have curfews or go on strike? The old lady laughed at him. She told him to leave the birds alone. Birds were lucky, she said. They could fly away from problems.

The road is dangerous. Every twenty minutes or so, a Rover comes roaring round the bends and Ken plunges, headfirst, with the other boys, into the roadside bushes. They lie low, dead-still, like mongooses, till the soldiers pass in a cloud of scattered pebbles.

The boys emerge, wary like crabs, of each other and the sounds that come on the wind from everywhere. Ken sidles with his friends — Tom, Stan and Sip — toward the ring of marbles.

The game is life; it must go on. The ring in which they've placed their marbles, is more important than the fear of soldiers on the road. It has become the world whose rules are fierce, where only winning matters.

No one feels this more than Sip who stands loose-mouthed counting his marbles. He flaunts them like some men would do their money; so that Ken and Stan and Tom begin to covet them.

Each is anxious to begin before the Rover returns and scatter them again. But Sip is taking his time.

'I have four new *ironies*,' he sings, lifting four highly-prized marbles made of steel, taken from the ball bearings of a car. The marbles shine in the sun like globes of light.

'How much *vainies* you have?' Ken asks, while his eyes narrow to needlepoints.

'Five,' answers Sip, blinking snakelike eyes.

Ken calculates quickly: a *vainy* equals two marbles, five *vainies* equal . . . .

'So you have ten,' Tom cuts in.

Ken sees the envy in the eyes of the others. He is more concerned about the passing Rovers. If only they would would stop, give him time! he would make a killing today.

Sip is still boasting, 'I have one big *tor.*' He shows an extra-large marble, three times the normal size. 'Dat wort' vainy — two! I have one jack's eye!' Sip holds out a very small marble one third the normal size. 'I have a vainy proper!' He lifts a cream, perfectly rounded stone. 'Dat wort two! Plus, I have six ord'nary ones; *not* counting the ironies.'

Ken shivers with anxiety. Tom and Stan are tense too because Sip does not play so well. He will fight them if they win his marbles, and take them all back. But Ken, Sip knows, does not fear him. He makes up for his smallness with his slingshot, tucked carefully inside the back pocket of his trousers. Ken could blind him anytime with a stone from his slingshot.

Stan hisses urgently, 'Le's play befo' dem soljers pass again.'

'Kay!' agrees Sip, and their faces relax in relief.

'You first, Tom. Rolls up!'

'Fat! You lose you' chance. You now, Sip. Then me.'

Ken wants Sip's marbles badly. He needs them, particularly the ironies. No way could he reveal his real reasons for wanting those steel marbles. If he tells his three friends the truth; that it is because of Dada, they would want to know more and he could not tell them more. Not now. Times like these, secrets are best kept locked in.

Because he must win, and is afraid the Rovers might return too soon, Ken says as casually as he could:

'We playin' till one of us go bust, right? No raafing — nobody grabbin' up dem marble wild-wild when the soljers pass. We play proper till somebody bust.'

Only Sip seems concerned. His snake's eyes grow dull. He frowns.

Ken adds quickly, 'If I win, I give back some.' He sends his marble crashing into the ring, collects the four that have been knocked out, kneels and pitches, missing deliberately the single remaining marble in the ring. Sip knocks it out and is encouraged to play on.

Ken is reflecting while he plays: in the evening, when the road becomes too hot to walk on with his naked feet, he will take the dirt-track through the bushes and the sugar canes of Hope Vale to visit Mrs. Ducan.

Mrs. Ducan has a very big concrete house, a pretty lawn, two cars and a tall fence of barbed wire that goes all the way round them. She also has a generator — a Delco — in a shed behind the house which gives light at night when all else is in darkness. Perhaps, he muses, if Dada had a fridge to store things in — like Mrs. Ducan — and a Delco to keep it going, he mightn't have desired Sip's marbles in the first case; nor would he be looking forward to visiting the Ducan's house that evening.

He will stand at the gate and call. Bo, the massive Alsatian, would come bounding viciously at him, snapping, shark-like, behind the iron bars of the gate. Or, Mrs. Ducan might call her dog before he leaps from the verandah, throw him a bone or something and with her nice voice, say: 'Stop it, Bo.' The dog will then follow her into the house and the lady, lock him in.

He will enter the gate only when Mrs. Ducan says to. Little Robby, her son, would most certainly be standing just in front of the big, glass door, watching him come up the driveway.

Mr. Ducan might not be in. He works for the government and drives on the road anytime he likes. The Rovers never stop him or shoot at him.

The lady will give Ken a small knife and, wordless, he will go behind the house, walk into the small swamp there and begin cutting calaloo leaves for her. He will cut until he has a bunch almost bigger than himself. The turkeys in the yard would crowd around and gobble curiously, shaking their long pink jowls at him.

Mr. Ducan loves turkeys; is so proud of them, he has given each one a name. He rears chickens too — Bantams — and has asked Ken many times to clean their coops for him. The turkeys have no coops; they guard the yard like dogs. Mrs. Ducan once said, her turkeys never sleep.

Indeed, at nights, before the curfew started, Ken used to see them strutting beneath the floodlight on the lawn.

'You bringsing!' snaps Sip.

Ken draws his hand a few inches back to appease the angry boy who is now losing all his marbles to him. The others are losing too but do not seem to mind.

Mrs. Ducan will pay him twenty five cents for cutting the calaloo and if he is lucky, some food wrapped in a piece of foil. She is doing him a favour. Mrs. Ducan always tells him that, just when he starts eating. And Little Robby's voice would chime in, 'That was *my* food; I ate that today.'

His mother will fondle him; ask him to be quiet, but Robby will go on; 'See where I bit that piece? There! There is where I bit.' Ken would smile, not minding him, because Robby is just three, plump, and very cute to play with. Mr. Ducan though, never seems too pleased when Ken tries to cuddle Robby. He'd even slapped the child once when he had boasted: 'My daddy has a gun — a big, big one!' But Mr. Ducan needn't have slapped Robby; everybody knew he had a gun.

'Last game,' growls Sip, aggressively.

''Kay,' says Ken whose pockets bulge with the marbles he has won.

A sudden blast of horns shatters the mid-morning calm. A Land Rover has come quietly coasting down the road. The boys just have time to fling themselves into the bushes and go pelting madly down the hill. The soldiers' laughter rise in the air and die with the passing of the vehicle.

Ken halts with his friends in the secure shade of a large mango tree at the foot of the hill. He gives back to each of the boys, a quarter of the marbles they have lost to him. Twenty remain in his pocket. Sip is not satisfied.

'Tha'z all?' he asks, sourly.

'Yep! I could give you back all of yours; even more!'

'Well, gimme then.'

'Nawwww!'

'You *say* you was goin' to gimme back all!'

'I never say so. And who the hell you bawlin' at! You can't fight me like you fight Tomo an' dem, yunno!'

'*Because* you have dat slingshot,' Sip retorts, derisively.

'Them green beas' soljers have gun! not so? Well *I* have slingshot; nothing wrong wit' dat. Lissen Sippo, we could make a bargin.'

'Yeh?' Sip grins, hopefully.

'Yep. You give me those four ironies, I give you all you' marbles back.'

'You crazy! Naw.'

'I give you fifteen — seven vainies, one extra.'

Sip's eyes narrow; they become mere slits. He looks more like a snake now than ever before.

'Eighteen,' Ken offers, fighting hard to hide his eagerness.

'Well, erm . . .' Sip is not too sure. He works his mouth like a fish.

'Twenty — no more. Ten vainies for four ole ironies. What you say?' Ken decides that if he has to fight Sip, he would have those steel marbles.

'Kay,' says Sip, surrendering grudgingly.

Stan is incredulous. '*Four* ironies!' he gapes. 'What you want *all* that ironies for Kenno?'

Ken smiles only with his lips. 'For me slingshot,' he says. 'Ironies better than stone to shoot with. You-all dunno that? Them round, them heavy — them is bullet, man. I can never miss if I shoot wit' ironies.'

'You plan to blind somebody?' Sip's hand creeps to his face, involuntarily. His eyes are dull with fear.

'Naw,' chuckles Ken. 'Don' 'fraid, man. Is meat I goin' shoot, da'z all. Nuff meat to last till strike over.'

The boys are very interested. They know their little friend hardly ever jokes.

'What meat you talkin' 'bout?' Tom wants to know.

'Jus' meat tha'z all. C'mon; I think I hear the old lady callin' me. Mebbe she want water o' somethin'. Le's go.'

The boys creep cautiously back up the hill, mystified more and more by their little friend's quietly spoken parables of big wire rings containing fat and feathered marbles that had somehow to be won.

****

There is a low moon over Hope Vale, big and yellow like
an over-ripe paw-paw. It hangs on the crest of Mont Airy
as if about to roll right down its slopes and burst at its
bottom.

Ken would have preferred if there were no moon, no
Rovers patrolling the night, no sound to listen out for
except the pit-pat-pattering of his own hurrying feet on
the slippery mud-path through the fields of sugar-cane.

The night is chill. He trembles because he walks
alone, dwarfed by the tall wind-tossed canes, glittering
silver in the moonlight. Above him is the road. Rovers
pass, their headlights sweeping mercilessly through the
night across the cane fields.

Dada does not know where he is now — three miles
away from home, hurrying fearfully through the canes,
surrounded by the cry of crickets, frogs and owls.

He told her he was going to the latrine a few yards
from the little house; that he would be some time there
since his gripe was very bad. She would be calling him
now, wondering why he was taking so long. She would
get no answer; would sit there in the dark listening and
waiting till he returned. Dada never complains. Tonight
however, she spoke of food — sustaining meat — like
something remembered, and it saddened him.

Several hours earlier, he visited Mrs. Ducan who
asked him to sweep the yard for her. The driveway was
packed with many big, bright cars.

Men in jackets and women in long, pretty dresses
were chatting and laughing in the verandah. They drank
from very slim glasses and poured their frothing drinks
from bright, green bottles with long, slender necks. Mrs.
Ducan pointed at her guests, explained that she was
busy and told him to leave when he had finished
sweeping. What a pretty lady she looked in her long blue
dress and the chain of pure, white beads around her
throat!

Bo barked at him from where he was chained beneath
the house. The big fat turkeys crowded around and
gobbled among themselves, polite and genteel, like the
people on the verandah. Only, they had no glasses to

drink from — mebbe because they didn't have no hands to hold them with, Ken thought.

Mrs. Ducan must have said something about him because two of the pretty-looking ladies looked at him. The one in red muttered something nice — he could see that by the way her lips moved and the smile she gave. But Mrs. Ducan gave him nothing. She was too busy with her friends.

Emerging from the cane fields, Ken finds himself at the foot of the hill on top of which stands the Ducan's house. He is no longer afraid; his mind is set.

The moon throws thick shadows wherever its light falls on objects all around. A chill wind comes up the valley from the Calivigny swamps, bringing the scent of crabs, frogs and rotting cane.

The boy pauses in the shade of a french-cashew tree; takes out his slingshot; tests it, feeling the power of the red rubber straps tense the muscles of his wrists, arms, shoulders, neck and back. He then takes the bird he shot that evening from where he has it wrapped under his shirt.

Ken wonders if the bird is enough to occupy Bo for the time he needs to accomplish his mission. Bo is not a small dog; with a single bite, he could snap off a boy's head, far less one stupid, little ground dove! Anyway, it was too late to turn back; he would have to chance it.

First, he must get through the barbed wire fence, crawl along the ground on his stomach — the way Sip said the soldiers did whenever they fought in wars. His target might be at the front of the house. It would therefore be more dangerous. If Bo doesn't get him, Mr. Ducan's gun may.

Ken flattens himself, inching his body beneath the lowest rung of wire. His mouth is raw with dirt, his stomach bruised with pebbles. But finally, he clears the fence. The Delco is putt-putting away. Hopefully, the Alsatian does not hear him. It is standing near the steps its nose pointing towards the fence. Ken thinks he hears the dog's deep growl, but it is too late; the fence would tear him to pieces if he tries to throw himself back out.

But why is Bo standing so still, sniffing the wind with his nose? Maybe he isn't sure, or he recognises Ken and is making up his mind.

The boy eases himself off the ground, swings his right arm high. The bird's small carcass goes sailing above his head and drops with a dull *plap!* just behind the dog. Bo barks viciously, just once. He turns suddenly to sniff the object on the ground. The dog lifts his head, sniffs again and still growling, takes the bird between his jaws and retreats beneath the house.

Swiftly, Ken creeps along the grass till he comes to the fringes of the lawn where the raw light falls full on him. He is beyond caring. His heart thumps painfully. His knees are shaking. But his hands are steady.

Crouching, he arms his slingshot. The five birds on the lawn seem to sense his presence. They lift their heads with sharp, jerky movements, chuckling among themselves, as they scan the perimeter of the fence. The tall gate is twenty feet to his right. The boy remembers the dog and fears it might soon come out, thirsting for more blood.

He aims the biggest bird and draws the powerful straps of the weapon back. He stretches the rubber until his arms tremble with the strain. He releases it suddenly.

Ken has shot the turkey exactly where he aimed — just behind the jowls. But all of a sudden, everything goes wrong. The bird does not lie still; it begins thrashing on the grass, raising a noisy, chuckling protest that brings the monstrous Alsatian rushing murderously from beneath the house.

The boy cannot run. He does not want to. He stays with his back against the barbed wire. The dog leaps at his face and, at the last moment, Ken throws himself aside. Bo's fearsome growl becomes a terrified yelp as his great weight crashes against the sharp wire. That is when Ken shoots him with his second marble. Bo screams a loud dog-scream, scrambles to his feet and, still yelping, bolts crazily for shelter beneath the house.

There is a stirring in the big house: chairs falling, a

man's deep voice thundering, lights going on in the rooms and a woman's whimpering. Ken thinks of Mr. Ducan's gun but does not move. He takes his third marble, aims the blazing bulb: fires. The light explodes in a shower of sparks and tinkling glass. Only the moon shines now; its light is soft on the grass.

The turkey is a dark heap where it has come to stop against the gate. Sprinting across the lawn, Ken lifts it; opens the gate, just managing to throw himself flat as the man comes out on the verandah.

Mr. Ducan stands silhouetted against the half-opened doorway. The gun is in his hand. He is shouting madly and looking confusedly into the night. Once again Ken aims his slingshot. It has his last marble. He aims carefully and fires. For the second time, the night explodes with the shattering of glass. This time it is the big door. The boy sees Mr. Ducan duck before throwing himself bodily inside the house.

The turkeys gobble, loudly. Bo yelps, pitifully. Ken, unsmiling, lifts his heavy load onto his small shoulders, and, in minutes, is on his way down the hill, bouncing with quick, cautious steps along the mud track, through the cane fields — a shadow among shadows.

The Return

I thought I understood why he claimed this spot which he came to, he said, each evening without fail. The hill was covered with tufts of long, coarse grass that smelt strongly of mint. They were sucked dry by the sun; bleached white, like the hair on my uncle's head.

I knew now why he always brought that mysterious odour of mint and musk the nights he came across our yard to sit, tight-faced, on my father's doorstep and eat my mother's food.

I was afraid of him — and my father too, I suspected — for uncle Dan was a such a silent man, that even when he spoke, you felt his words were coming from some deep, dark place within, like clean water dripping from a cave — sounds that made the silence stronger. I always thought of him like that.

We were watching the sun go down behind the sea. It did not sink quietly, as I often used to see it do from my home several miles away. Now, there were no smoky-blue hills standing between the sun and us; just the big, wide sea. It seemed to hang there, battling hotly to keep its place just above the restless water. The wind came in hard, harsh gasps and threw the scent of raw seaweed and mangrove in our faces. The sky was bleeding colours I had never dreamt of before. They trickled down into the vast, tossing expanse of wind, and water, staining it in the exact patterns of the sky above us, till I could not tell the difference between sky and sea. I looked into my uncle's face; saw that his eyes had become luminiscent like glass, reflecting everything. A person felt uneasy just sitting there with him.

I wondered what people would think if they saw us there on the hill above the precipice that dropped straight down to the sea. I knew what my father would have done, having warned me many times to stay clear of my uncle, Dan, who had so often offered to take me to the sea with him. Indeed, I could not understand my father's silence or my mother's fear when, after studying the distant, blue patch between the hills, I asked them about the sea. How was it made? Where did it lead to? Why was it blue? What made it roar like that — so distant yet so powerful — especially when wind blew hard and rain fell? And, above all, why did they take everyone else there: my brothers, sisters — everyone else but me?

I began to feel deeply troubled, remembering the things I had heard about my uncle. My parents sometimes spoke about him — in half-whispers — when they thought I wasn't listening. In vain, I would struggle to make sense of the snatches of conversation I overheard. There were some words that came over and over again: *Bella . . . . nice child . . . . son, Carlo, bad way . . . water . . . crazy . . . dead . . . pity 'bout Dan!*

It had taken me several months of determined listening and great efforts of the imagination before I could finally fit those words into a sensible whole. The words were no more than a sort of drawing to which I added my own colour. But I was at peace again with myself.

'Uncle Dan!'

He didn't hear me. Was staring, still as a stone, across the lagoon where he'd said the foreigners came and moored their yachts. I followed his stare beyond the massive procession of breakers that rose snarling, and thundered frighteningly against Blue Reef, to the islet just beyond the raging waves. Perhaps, I mused, he was thinking about what he had done to me that very afternoon.

He'd taken me over to the little island in what he said was his friend's boat. I became sick with terror when, half-way there, the small tub began to toss and roll as if it had a life of its own.

My uncle spoke casually about the sharks and barracudas he'd hauled up from the depths beneath us, and the powerful evening tides that could sweep a boat beyond the horizon in minutes — all the way to Venezuela. But it was still afternoon, he assured me, and hopefully, we would return before the tide came in.

He showed me the house on the island where he said the white man lived. I asked him which white man.

'The funny one,' he replied, glaring at me with discouraging eyes.

The house was only a skeleton, windowless and crumbling; gutted, it seemed, by a terrible fire because the stone walls were black and cracked in many places. The rafters and joists were eaten away by the same fire. But it must have been a massive house — from its tall decaying walls to the concrete path that led down to the small jetty.

A frightening place, I thought, for a man to live in. A small, green world of wind and birds; of sand and stones and coconut trees. Despite the sun, a cold world — just beyond the mainland, yet miles away. A place for crabs and lizards.

My uncle stood in the boat, supporting his weight with both oars. He was contemplating the dead building so intensly, I forgot where I was and became lost too.

He startled me, 'You could swim?'

'Naww,' I answered

'You 'fraid de sea?'

'Nuh, well — lil' bit.'

He threw me out, then. Before I could realise what was happening he caught me in his grip and dumped me bodily into the water. I sank screaming. Then my voice was cut off by the water. I surfaced drinking air and liquid salt. Kicking wildly, I reached for the boat. He pushed me back with an oar, his commands coming flat, merciless: 'Use your goddam hand and foot. Don' stop movin' jus' beat de water.'

I kept screaming; reached for the boat again, grabbing air as the oar sent me down. I surfaced, saw him dimly against the sky standing over me, and began thrashing the water, finding myself turning every which way.

'Thaa'z right! Keep it up, Sonny. You fadder take too damn long to send you.'

I kept it up and found my panic being replaced by cautious delight as I realised I was not sinking but actually swimming! — wildly, awkwardly; but swimming. Still somewhat fearful, I began to like the way the water made my skin tingle. I promised myself afterwards to do this again, sometime — perhaps alone.

'Uncle Dan?'

'Uh?'

The gulls were stark against the bleeding sky. Their distressed cries came sharp on the wind.

'Uncle Dan, who is Bella?'

'A girl — a girl I used to know. Why?'

'She was crazy?'

'Nuh. She not here no more.' He was looking at me curiously. I felt as if I had to answer his questioning stare.

'Mummy talk as if she — well, I dunno. Thought she was a nice child — a gyul who was in a bad way and was crazy, cause she had a son.'

'You modder tell you dat?'

'She didn' tell me; I hear dem. Yunno, I never hear everything; only piece-piece.'

The way he was looking at me made me nervous. I thought he was going to lift me and throw me over the cliff below, into the sea. This time he wouldn' need an oar to keep me off. The tide would see to that.

'What I could tell you?' He'd asked as though he didn't expect an answer.

I shrugged, preparing myself to be lifted and thrown. Instead, he began to uproot the grass between his knees, exposing the dryness of the chalky soil under us.

'What esle they say?'

'Nuffing. They say you lil' crazy. You crazy fo' true?'

'You think so?'

'Uhm, nuh; not really — just a li'l bit, sometimes.' My uncle chuckled — a dry sound, like twigs crackling.

'Okay, so I crazy to come here every evenin' to wait fo' dem.'

'Who?'

'Bella and me son.'

'Cousin Carl?'

'You mother tell you 'bout that too?'

'I hear you had a son name Carl; he dead, not so?'

'He not dead! Is why I come here to wait for 'im.'

I wished I hadn't started prying. At least *my* version was more coherent.

'Where cousin Carl is now?'

'Over there — somewhere.' My eyes followed his finger which seemed to be pointing way beyond the horizon.

'In a boat?'

'No swimmin'. Next mont' make it fifteen years.'

'Dat don' make no sense. I don' unnerstan'.'

'If you stop interuptin' me, I might agree to tell you. Is a big world — you know dat? The older you get, the more you realise how different things is and how strange. Is a long story. You wouldn' tell nobody if I tell you? You lissenin!?'

'Uh? Yeh-yeh-yeh!' In fact, I had been trying to figure out how a person could be swimming for fifteen years. I mean, you couldn't light no fire in the sea to cook; unless, cousin Carl ate raw fish. Wasn't he tired of swimming after fifteen years? *I* was dead tired after less than three minutes in the water.

'Your cousin, Carl, uses to lissen. And he never butt in when I talkin'!'

He must have been stupid then, I thought, contemptuously. Uncle must have heard my thoughts:

'Carl was a smart boy. Intelligent. Quiet and gentle as water — a bit like you. Was November-born same like you. A rain-season child. He got fed up o' waitin' to see the worl' so he decide to born after seven mont's. Always like to have hi' own way.

'Hi' mother had a child before 'im — a li'l girl name Bella. Wasn' my daugther, but I treat 'er like me own. Pretty! You never see a li'l girl so pretty. She was one year older dan Carl.

'Even from small, we realise dat someting was funny

'bout dem. Dey uses to stick so close togedder — real
close! I uses to watch dem sometimes and have the
strange feelin' dat dey wuz de same person; only she
wuz de woman part o' he; or he, de man part o' she. You
unnerstan?'

'Yeh,' I muttered. But I didn't understand; not really.

'Dey had a love for water dat nobody could unnerstan'. From birt', Bella an' Carl love water. I 'member de
times we uses to bathe dem. Was strange: most times
you put children in water, dey start cryin'; Bella an' Carl
start crying' when you *take* dem out! De first time we
bring dem to de river was as if dey reach home. A little
time later, dey dissappear and we start searchin' fo'
dem, frighten like hell. Jeeezan, man! We search fo' dem
chil'ren for hours, t'inking dat de worst happen. We
nearly get crazy. Guess where we find dem! Hah! — in a
big, deep pool far down de river, swimmin.' Yes! Bella
and Carl swimmin' around and laughin' like two likkle
mullet. I bus' dey tail good — I was so damn vex — but I
hurt me head for a long-long time afterwards wonderin'
how dem two chil'ren learn to swim so good 'cause
nobody never teach dem. How?'

My uncle had stopped pulling the grass; seemed to be
talking to the sea.

'De years pass quick — so quick it catch me sort of
unawares to see how big Carl and Bella get. Bella grow
like a piece o' sugar cane — all slim an' smooth an' wavy-
like. She wuz so pretty, I uses to close me eyes after
seein' 'er and feel 'fraid for she. Real 'fraid 'cause I see
how stupid an' speechless she make dem boys 'come
and I tell meself, 'Dano, dat aint good — de girl have
power over people.'

'Growin' up didn' seperate 'er from Carlo, like it
oughter. After a time, children should go deir own ways.
Is natral. But dem — naaah! Dem get closer; so close,
dey stop talk to one anudder!'

Uncle must have seen my puzzlement. He explained:

'You see, they didn' have no need to; dey start talkin'
wid dey face — yes-yes, dat's what I say — dey face! Dey
would siddown for hours below de plum tree across de
yard. She would watch 'im an' he watch 'er back, talkin-

like. Den you see dem shake deir head an grin as if dey
agree to somethin' and so on — laughin' an' talkin'
widdout a single word, for hours!'

'People uses to watch dem an' shoo-shoo about it
because Bella and Carl wuz brodder an' sister — come
from de same modder — an *dat* kind o' frien'ship not
good to encourage. But nobody could stop dem. We try
everyt'ing to break dem up: I beat dem, cuss dem,
threaten dem, but was as if I was tyin' dem tighter
togedder. Dey jus' go an' sit under de plum tree an' cry
an' start comfortin' each odder wid deir face-talk.'

'Is a love story?' I ventured.

'Is no damn story, man; I speakin' de gospel trut',
Sonny. What happen, you don' believe me?'

'Uh-huh.'

'Well, I t'ink is two tings dat start de trouble; but
sometimes I feel dem born wid it inside dem — like how
dem born fo' water. You see, some people born wid deir
own trouble inside dem. De same t'ing dat make dem big
and strong is what does break dem down to nothing
afterwards. People start makin' Bella know how pretty
she was. I know a man — I never learn hi' name — who
uses to come from de city, drive all de way in hi' shiny,
black car just to watch at Bella; not even to talk to her.
She must ha' been fourteen then, just fourteen an' she
had all dis power.

'De girl start pesterin' her modder for money to buy
woman-t'ings: costlimetics an' perfume an' so on. We
never had no money to give 'er. Carlo was de same; he
start askin' fo' t'ings for hi' sister too. He uses to ask me
— never hid nothin' from me, dat boy! Is how I know he
an' Bella wuz planning to go overseas to become a
model-queen o' somethin'. And he, he didn' know what
he want; long as dey wuz togedder. I never take dem
serious though.'

'Is around dat time dey start goin' to de sea. I never
know how or when it start. Is a fisherman — a friend —
who make me know. Every evenin, Carl an' Bella would
dissappear. I uses to t'ink it was — well, you find young
people hidin' all over de place sometimes; so I thought

was dat. Anyway, de man tell me he see dem every evenin' swimmin' across dere!' Uncle Dan pointed at the churning expanse of water. 'Dere, across dat bad-water to the li'l islan' where de house is!'

'But de tide!'

'Yes! An' dem big white breakers across dere and de sharks. You unnerstan' why I thought de fisherman was lyin 'bout my children? But it was true. I dunno how Bella an' Carlo uses to do it. It wasn' human to walk five miles from home an' swim quite across dat nasty water every evenin' *an'* return home — de two of dem togedder — as if dem just come from strollin' across de yard. I hear odder people talkin', so I decide to see fo' meself.

'I stand up right dere one evenin'. He was pointing at the samll bay to our right. 'What I see was two black spots bobbing up an' down, up an' down way over dere past dem breakers, in de middle o' de tide. All you could see wuz deir head, side by side, heading fo' de islan'.

'Nobody never had no control over dem; not oven deir modder. Is like de kind o' children you have nowadays. If dey want to have deir way, you cyahn' stop dem; dey radder dead firs'. But I learn somethin' dat evenin': I learn where Bella an' de boy get those ideas in deir head about model-queen an' overseas an' all dat from. You see, it had dis white man come from America, livin' in dat house on de islan'. He buy dat islan'; carry over every piece o' board, every nail! an' buil' dat house dere. Had a long, white boat too, wit' sail, like wings.'

'De two chil'ren use to cross dat water an' go to dat man. Sudden so, dem start gettin strange. Use to hear dem talkin 'bout San Francisco, bourbon, whisky on de rocks, car, TeeVee an' movin' pictures.'

'You *hear* dem talkin' wid deir face?' I asked.

'Naw, wid deir mout'. I tell you dey wuz gettin' strange; not so? Wuz just a feelin', but I start t'inkin dey wuz hidin' a lot o' t'ings from us. As if de tings dem tell us 'bout wuz in deir head, but wuz so real to dem, dey couldn' see nothin' else around dem.'

'It continue-it continue-it continue, till one day Bella

leave *befo'* Carl come home from school — he was goin'
Secondry an' he come home latish sometimes. She just
dissappear. An' de nex evenin' was de same t'ing, an' de
nex, an' de nex, and de nex. When Carlo reach home, was
as if he was lost: he just keep lookin' around 'im daze-
like, till it hit 'im dat she was really gone widdout 'im. I
watch 'im take up hi' t'ings an' leave widdout eatin'!
widdout a word.'

'You never try to stop dem?' I wanted to know. I
couldn't help wishing I had the kind of freedom that
Bella and my cousin, Carlo, seemed to have enjoyed.

'Stop dem! You could stop storm from comin'? I try
everyting, but it didn' make no sense.'

'I start noticin' dat Bella use to leave just after I hear a
boat-horn comin distant-distant from de sea. Toooooot-
tooooot! an' then she leave soon after. Was de white man
'boat callin' her before Carlo could return from school.
Sunday, Saturday, everyday, come rain or shine she
make sure she leave home before the boy. But dey
always return togedder.'

Uncle Dan paused for breath. The sky was smoulder-
ing. His eyes reflected it — a dying fire.

'It must ha' been five month after, dat Bella begin to
bring home nice t'ings — clothes, shoes, watch, ring
chain — all kinds o' t'ings. Carlo bear it real patient, but
I know dat even stone does break; just keep poundin' it
regular an' it must crack one day. A time come when he
stop' follow 'er to de sea. He would stand an' watch 'er,
sort of helpless, get up an' leave after de boat call.
Somethin' was sufferin inside o' dem because you could
se how it hurt when dey pullin' away from each odder
sort of. You tired, Sonny?'

'Naw! What happen?'

'He stop talk to 'er.'

'He never use to!'

'I mean face-talk.'

'Uh-huh; what happen after?'

'He start talkin to her again.'

I sat up. 'How come?'

'She got sheself in big trouble. I dunno for sure; but I

believe so. One evenin' Bella come back home and went straight below de plum tree. Was a way o' tellin' Carlo, she want to talk to 'im. Dey wuz outside till past midnight. Next day wuz de same t'ing. I had de feelin' dey was arguin, mostly wid deir face. But now an' den, you would hear 'im say: *'No! No!'* like somet'ing hurtin' 'im — and she, sayin', cry-cry-like: *'Is your fault you shouldn' ha' bring me dere!'* And he sayin': *'Sorry.'* And so on and so forth.'

'I thought that mebbe de white man wuz goin' away wit' her after throwin' gravel in me son rice. Dat was how it sound to me. But de boat call every day for a long time and Bella never go nowhere. She wait for Carl to come home an' start sufferin' wit' her. And no matter how much I ask, dem never tell me nothin'.

'Is about a mont' after, I realise what the problem wuz. I start seein' signs.'

'What signs?'

'Jus' signs,' he snapped back. 'But she couldn' carry it — no way! I don' think she did want to either. Somebody tell me de white man lef' wit' he boat all of a sudden. Perhaps she realise dat de closest she would ever get to be a model-queen in America was wot was happenin' to her.'

'Wuz a hard time for two of 'em — a hard time for us too, cause dey couldn' get dis San Francisco thing out o' deir head. I dunno what de man show dem, but it catch dem for good. Eatin' up deir insides, sort of.

'I t'ink I know when dey come to de decision 'cause dem stop arguin' an' start lookin' happy again — kind o' clean — like a person who just wash mud off deir face. Is weeks later I realise what de decision was.'

'Dey got up one mornin', put on deir best Sunday-clothes and left. I was glad 'cause dey wuz so happy again. Dey tell us dey goin' be back evenin'-time; dey need a bit o' time togedder. Dat make me laugh! An' — guess what dem do?'

'Church?'

'Naw. Sea! Somebody bring deir clothes for me de next day — everyt'ing dey did put on dat mornin', dey

leave behind. De person say how he see dem swimmin'
past de islan', out, out past dem breakers; swimmin' till
de distance hide dem from hi' eyes.'

'Dey drown?'

'Nawww!' My uncle growled, impatiently. 'Dem is
water-children, I tell you. Dem can't drown 'cause dey
could swim better dan fish. Dey say dey wuz comin' back
evenin' time but dey didn' say *which* evenin'. You
unnerstan? So I believe dey swimmin' still.'

I looked up in wonderment, respect. *'Fifteen* years!?'

'Yup! Is not a long time if you check how big de world
is. It make sense, you know.' Uncle Dan was smiling.
'You see, de world is round like a orange — I read it in
one o' Carlo' book. Dat mean, if you start swimmin' from
here and continue right on widdout stoppin', you must
come back to de same place after a time because is
'round you goin'. You believe me?' He seemed worried.
'A man must believe, you know; else it don't make no
sense livin'.'

I assured him that I believed and was looking forward
to seeing cousin Carlo and Bella one day.

'And de white man?' I asked. 'He gone back to
America for true?'

'More o' less. I uses to wish he didn' never come. Take
my children mind wit' him. But he cyah come back; I see
to dat.'

'How?'

'One night de house burn down; a accident — bad,
real bad!'

'You . . .'

'Yeh. C'mon, Sonny; sun gone down: it gettin' late. I
don' t'ink dat Bella an' Carlo goin' reach back dis
evenin'. Mebbe tomorrow.'

He took my hand and led me down the hill.

The Understanding

Something is wrong with you. They keep telling you that because you think it's so much better outside and crave madly to rush to your feet, leap over their heads, kicking them down, and everything else in your path; because you burn to break through the iron door and go flying across the yard, over the wire fence and into the sun.

What will they say if you tell them that this month, now the rains are over, is the month the rainbirds sing their last songs and the yam-shoots, redder than blood from a fresh-cut finger will soon come snaking from the black earth?

If only they could listen, they would hear the garden-people chopping in the deep bush; the sound, like heartbeats, coming, going, coming again over the cane-fields, up and beyond the river-valley. Like you, they won't need to close their eyes to imagine — when the wind comes — that the trees, the grass, the vines are living, breathing things that talk among themselves of this, the rich time of warm earth and new leaves.

The river will be bright with sunshine; and the stone, cool, on which you love to sit and watch the girls come — on Fridays mostly — to laugh and tease and do their laundering.

The girls like to make fun of you — the boys too, who gather like blackbirds on the bank to stare at Ela, Jenny, Sara, Pansy . . . standing wet and almost bare in the pools, pounding clothes on stone.

Then it is the bigger boys who come racing through the *sigin'* and wild calaloo. They chase the Blackbirds off. But you, they leave alone as they wrestle on the bank among the water-grass and shout in men's voices.

In the pools, they create a storm around the girls, splashing white water, fishing among the stones; their real reason, to draw close to the girls and fondle them all over. Then the waterfights would begin in earnest.

'Behave!' the girls would scream. Now, they no longer laugh like girls; they laugh like women and leave their washing floating on the water.

'Behave!' they squeal.

Yet, Ela leaves the water and goes with Carl. She resists, laughing as he tugs her along. They go through the guavas, past the tall breadnut tree, up where the black sage tie their branches together and form cool, leafy caves. Ela's woman-laugh comes loud and clean above the bush. Then silence — except for the *cee-cee* birds', the *johnnyheads'* and the *pikayoes'* cheep-cheep-cheeping among the foliage.

Jenny follows Masso; Sara, Sam: until they are all gone, leaving ugly Polo standing unhappy guard on the bank, his miserable eyes on Pansy who never looks up from her washing.

You used to wonder: what made the girls go? What happened there in the quiet where the vines hang down from the cutlet trees like a great green waterfall?

It was Pansy who made you know one day when, with no one else present, she woman-laughed; began teasing you. Why, she asked, did you always sit on the same ole riverstone, dumb like makookoo, and just watch the world run away? She said it nice and friendly, so you answered her. And she, pretty with her smile, was surprised.

You told her that the world never ran away if a person held tightly on to it; it just took them along with it. She laughed, which made you brave enough to go to her and take her hand.

You were both afraid: Pansy, because she had never before gone up the bank, through the guavas, past the breadnut tree and into the silence of the vinefall; you, because you had always gone there alone.

Nothing more should be said about this, really. Only

that you were ashamed. It was not like in the book Steve had lent you. You did not feel — as others did — to boast. More dissappointingly, there was not the expected miracle of becoming suddenly grown up afterwards. Your voice did not change and you had not grown taller. Was that why Pansy could not look at you; nor you, her? Was that why you never spoke to each other since?

Still, you like the river and your favourite stone. So different they are from this hateful place with its smell of ink, paper, old furniture; the scratch-scratch-scratching of chalk on board, pen on paper; and voices! — the endless hive of whispering, whimpering, tittering voices you cannot shut out, even in your dreams.

But you cannot leave here. Mammy, when she finds out, will be merciless. She will skin you alive. Mammy always finds out.

Each day, she comes from work, sets her tray down and asks, 'You went to school today, Tony?'

'Yes, Ma.'

'Show me what you do today, then.'

She looks at the notebook, squinting her eyes fiercely. She does not read or write but Ma knows that a red X means you got it wrong and a tick across the page is what you ought to have there.

No fresh writing means simply, you did not go to school. So she takes the whip out and, while thrashing, complains that she is killing herself for a mere pittance on the government' road; that she has to swallow everyone's abuse — children's and adult's alike, who call her, scornfully, a 'travaux.' And what for? — one useless child who prefers to dreeveway rather than put some learning in his head. A child "toobesides", whose father was a nastiness that left her heavy with him and went off with some other jamette who does not know how to wash her own face!

To avoid learning and Mammy's heavy hand, therefore, you sometimes write anything on the notebook, borrow Steve's red pen and cover the page with ticks. If need be, you write your teacher's signature: Mr. C. Celestine!

Your father, who is he? You cannot make a picture in your mind. Though Mammy, tired in the evenings after work, sits describing him in detailed cursings. She stares into the roof as if he live up there and curses him until she falls asleep on the chair. You do not miss him, though. You have many fathers — all the tall, nice-looking men you see on your way to school. You watch them closely, give them a voice, dress them as it pleases you and they are your Dads whenever you want, for however long you want.

Mr. Celestine could never become your father. He never smiles; is happy only when his leather strap is crashing down on some poor pupil's behind. Besides, he can't have children because he has only one seed, instead of the natural two. This might not be true though, since the boys who say this do not like him. They do no like any teacher who could make them shut up with just one glance.

But there must be a reason why he is always so full of anger. He brings it with him in the morning, spills it out on the class and, at lunchtime, goes back home to refill. He is hungry-thin — no one ever sees him eat — and he shuts himself up in his office for long hours after school.

He hates you. Else, why does he look at you as though you are a fly sitting on the edge of his ruler?

You still remember the morning he read to the class that English Comprehension passage.

In the story, Tarvy and Jane had cereal with milk, toast with butter and eggs, for breakfast. Mr. Celestine spent half the morning talking about balanced diets as though they were to be found on the ground everywhere.

'What did some of us have?' he asked the class.

Most of the class had bread and eggs and milk. Most of the class were lying! He came to you, finally:

'Anthony Skinner. Skinner! Yes, you! Wake up, boy! I asked you what you had for breakfast?'

'Ham and egg and bacon, Sir! And wholemeal bread!'

Mr. Celestine looked into your face and smiled as though he could see the two, green bananas boiled in salted water, and the plain black sage tea you had consumed that morning. He smiled but silenced the class savagely when they started laughing.

Now you really want to escape because soon the bell will ring and Mr. Celestine will collect the test he has asked the class to do.

You have not done the test. The papers lie untouched before you. Instead, you have chosen to do yesterday's assignment — the composition he had belted you for not doing because you were in a mood for reading Geography then. He would not want yesterday's work. In fact, he will murder you when he finds that you have not done the Maths Test; that for some strange reason, you felt compelled to write the composition.

The task, for the first time, is an attractive one.

'Honesty,' Mr. Celestine had said, 'is the hallmark of good writing, so, keeping in mind the Queen's English, I want you people to write about anything you like. Just be honest about it.'

Now, yesterday's assignment lies almost complete before you. The test, untouched.

Mr. Celestine has begun to collect the test. He must not see what you have written about Pansy, Ela, Jenny . about the river calling, your mother staring at your father in the ceiling, about Mr. Celestine himself! Quickly, you put the three pages of the composition together, begin to tear them apart, like this . . .

'Hold it there, Skinner,' Mr. Celestine's voice cuts like a knife.

'Sir?'

'Why are you tearing up the test. Are you mad?' His eyes are very hard. He has forgotten the rest of the class and is approaching. You *have* to get rid of the composition!

'I said hold it, Skinner! Let me see what you are doing there.'

'Nothing, Sir.'

'Nothing! You call tearing up your Maths Promotion Test 'nothing'?'

But he'd never said it was a Maths Promotion Test!

'Come, come, come! Let me see what you are not satisfied with. Pass those pages.'

Mr. Celestine snatches the torn pages, looks at them a long time and becomes very, very confused. 'Something

is wrong with you!' he reads. 'They keep telling you that.
. . .' The bell rings. He stops.

'He manages to say, 'O.K. class. You heard the bell.
Stop staring at me as if it's the end of the world —
though it might well be for you, Mr. Skinner! The rest of
you leave your work on my desk and file *out*, you hear
me? File out in an orderly manner! I do not want
anybody from this class hanging around my office. You
will proceed there, Sir Anthony Skinner and wait till I
come. I advise you to pray for your personal deliverance
while you wait. Now move!'

'Sir . . . .'

'I SAY MOOOVE!!'

'Yessir.'

*   *   *   *

The office is quiet, white; small. A single desk neatly
stacked with paper. It smells of books and reams of
bristol board. On the far wall, a single picture of a small
boy clutching a gift of dried flowers.

'Sit down, boy!' Mr. Celestine is sitting at the desk.
The strap is in his right hand.

'Skinner, what is the problem?'

'No problem, Sir.'

'You call playing the arse in class 'no problem'?'

'No, Sir.'

'Well what is the problem then!'

'No problem, Sir.'

'You realise you spoil your chances for promotion to
scholarship class?'

'You didn't say it was a promotion-test, Sir.'

'I don't have to *say* so.' Mr. Celestine's right hand
convluses angrily.

'I suppose you expect me to write the answers on the
blackbord for you too?'

'No, Sir.'

'Well then, whats happening to you, man! Like you
gone stupid or something. You do everything wrongside: you walk wrongside, you think wrongside, you even
look wrongside! Sit up! And button up your shirt

properly! Look at those fingernails, Jeeeez! Your hair comb?'

'Yessir.'

'I have a good mind to spend this hour lacing you. But licks don't make no difference to you. You are Tarzan himself. Like your skin harder than this strap, right?'

'No, Sir'

Jeeez! You miss that by a nook.

Mr. Celestine continues, 'I don't know why the hell I so concerned about you . . .'

'Me, Sir?'

'Shut up!' Mr. Celestine gets up, walks a few yards from his desk and stands looking angrily at the closed door. The room is filled with his anger, he reseats himself and stares accusingly. 'If you were stupid I wouldn't mind. I wouldn't even look at you twice. I know what the problem is: you are ashamed! That's what. Don't think I don't know. You watch the children with shoes on, then look at your own bare feet and feel the world is owing you a pair. Since when a new pair of shoes becomes equal to how well you perform in class!'

'I didn't say so, Sir.'

'Shut up!'

'Sir.'

'You refuse to come first in class — like is a responsibility you 'fraid. Don't look at me like that! You damwelly know you wasting yourself, letting those shoes in class frighten you into playing the jack-ass. You think they don't know it! Ask yourself why they keep flashing them in front of you so! — to dazzle you. Look at me! You think I was all that different from you?' Mr. Celestine dawdles with the strap. He does not speak for a long while, then:

'So the class don't like me?' He speaks as though he couldn't care less.

'Well, Sir . . . uhm . . . You see, I won' really say so. They jus' a lil' bit 'fraid of you.'

Mr. Celestine smiles. He plays with the strap and looks at the picture on the wall — the boy with the dried flowers.

'Amazing,' he says to the picture. 'Truly amazing! Where did you learn to write like that?'

The picture doesn't answer.

'I ask you a question, Skinner!'

'Sorry, Sir. You mean the composition? Dunno. It just come. I write and it just come.'

'I,' no — 'You!' You wrote in the second person singular! 'You told her that the world never runs away if a person held tightly onto it. It just takes him along.' You believe that?'

'Yessir.'

'I had faith like that once.' Mr. Celestine speaks to the picture on the wall. 'But now, I don't know. I jus' dunno. Listen, Skinner, don't repeat this, but your crazy composition — that you should have done *yesterday* — was more useful to me than the whole damn Maths test. And to think I was beginning to dislike you. You know that?'

'No .'

'You hungry?'

It is less embarrassing to leave the question un-answered. Mr. Celestine takes a small, plastic container from his bag. He pauses a long moment then, with a strange smile, he opens it. Inside, there is saltfish and green bananas steamed in coconut juice!

'Here, Skinner! Have some of my ham and eggs and bacon with wholemeal bread!' The room is filled with the sudden, loud pleasure of a joke shared in secrecy.

The food is good; the odour, sweet, stirring hunger.

'Listen, Skinny,' Mr. Celestine laughs and licks his fingers. He seems happy to have someone licking fingers with him. 'Hear this! Next year I will be teaching scholarship-class. It means I have you fools for two years straight. When I finish, you-all will be as sharp as cutlass on grinding stone. *You* will pass, even if I have to kill you to make you do it. Because *I* want the island scholarship; and you, mister-man, will get it for me. Then it will be my chance for Teacher's College; and after, University. They can't refuse my application if I get the best results. Five years in this place is enough. A man must move on. I want to go. Go! That is why I don't want no children and not for *any* other reason, you understand?' Mr. Celestine's eyes are black and reproachful.

'Yes, Sir.'

'So no more jumping around on riverstones and bushes with little Miss Fancy or whatever-her-name-is. You catch me? From now on is books, books, books and more books! Agreed? Now come shake hands because this is an understanding between us — a contract if you like. You get the Island Schol' and I get what I want . . .'

The food was nice. A pity there wasn't more. There should have been more. His hands are warm, firm — like a father's should be.

'Take this envelope. Give it to your mother. DON'T OPEN IT! Give it to her and tell her to buy a good pair of shoes, a real shirt and a pair of long pants. Some underwear too. I don't want to see all your spare parts sticking out at everyone anymore. Now get out of my office before I do something crazy with this strap!'

'By the way, if the class want to know what happened. Tell them I near tear the skin off you. Stop grinning at me, Skinner.'

'Yessir.'

'And do me a favour, man. When you get outside, go to the standpipe and wash the mud off your feet seeing as school really begin for you on Monday.'

'Yes, Mr. Celestine.'

'Now . . . er, before you go, tell me, little man: why doesn't the class like me?'

'Well, Sir, they don't know you like I know you now.'

'Who! You? You know me!' Mr. Celestine is suddenly very angry.

'No-no, Sir — uhm, I don't know you. I don' know you at all.'

'Good. Go on — and close the door behind you. Er, Skinner?'

'Sir?'

'Don't let nobody fool you, son; there's nothing wrong with you. And thanks, thanks a lot, Skinner. Go on!'

Mr. Celestine does not seem to hear the door closing. He is grinning angrily at the picture on the wall.

The Kite

'You goin' and fly kite but make sure you come back as you goin', no confusion, hear?' His mother stood in the doorway wiping her wet hands on her frock.

Ian looked up quietly, 'I never look for confusion.'

'You never have to *look* for it; it does come and meet you right where you is. Those stinkers up there have nothing else to do but make confusion.' She raised her head sharply, sniffed and hurried back into the kitchen. Metal clanged against metal and a small cloud of steam gushed through the kitchen window.

Ian busied himself with his kite. He folded the tail, carefully balling the two strips around his hand. Not a knot on these tails! He had dug endlessly among the old clothes and bedding until he had finally discovered a tattered sheet — a wonderful thing! And Lord! with what loving fingers had he stripped it into neat, smooth bands for his kite.

Lordy, what a kite; never a kite like this one! Making it himself, it was a miracle of creation. No ordinary flex had gone to make this kite. He had searched for the thickest, the straightest, the best materials for his kite — a five mile hunt under the coconut trees round about; leaving home as early as the sun allowed and taking the goat for tying out — a convenient excuse.

It was down by the swamp where the river met the sea and you could actually smell the water and the crabs; it was among those dark bushes he found the right coconut tree..

Back home, Mama's knife and the packet of razor blades were all he needed. The knife was for cleaning away the straw from the flex. And the razors, he had bought them, saving cent by cent until he had enough money. These were for shaving the flex clean and smooth. He had borrowed Ma's thread, and kept his mouth closed tightly when she began to wonder about it; even helping her search in the corners where it might have fallen and lodged. Of course Ma never found it.

Ian had made the frame, measuring and re-measuring, gauging and re-gauging, carefully, so that the kite would have 'balance'. One cross-piece, two side-pieces, then the compass-head: put them together with caution and bind them tight until it stood there before him — the kite — framed in thread — a perfect hexagon. Pull on the thread and tighten it so that the kite would have 'belly' and will not 'capute' or turn over and wobble when it was flying.

It was Mama who had bought the long spool of thread and the pretty-paper. Mama had also boiled the starch for him; but he had rooted and grated and strained the manioc himself, carefully, because she warned him many times that manioc was poison.

And he made the kite that very night. While Ma went to sleep, he worked — never more loving, never more careful in all his life.

Now it was time to fly. Today, Good Friday, all the boys were up there on the hill with their kites. Two weeks since, he had made it, rising each morning, inspecting it for roach-bites. None! The same ceremony each night, before bed — the first and final thing he did each day.

Holding the kite up against the sun, the paper — red and mauve and gold and green — was beautiful and glowing. The silver stars he had stuck on it, those he took from cigarette cartons, made sparks where the sun fell on them. Lordy, watch at a kite! *Never* a kite like this in all the world. The joy and excitement bubbled over in Ian and it came out in a proud, long laugh; so that Ma, in her own serious way, called out pleasantly from the kitchen.

'Go 'long and 'joy yourself boy. 'Member to fly you kite for yourself. Don't lend, don't borrow, don't give no feel and don't feel nobody else kite 'cause that bring confusion and accident. No cussing! Today is GOOD Friday. Stay for yourself. That way, kite thread won't get tied up and nobody won't bus' your kite. I's getting old but me and your deceased father was children too and in *we* days the saying was, 'Kite is fight' and that ain't change no way.'

Still feeling good, Ian bawled out, 'Going stay by meself, Ma. Going behave myself real good. I not feelin' nobody kite and nobody goin' feel mine. I not cussing neither. You's getting old but you's . . .'

'Boy! You mocking me?' The voice was stern but flecked with laughter.

'No Ma! I gone, I comin' home early.'

'Better has, or . . .'

'Kay!'

Ian climbed the hill as fast as the kite would allow him. He held it delicately above his head, slowing to a crawl wherever he met small obstacles, especially dried branches. They could destroy a kite in a wink, punching through the soft 'pretty-paper' and mauling it to shreds, leaving only a bare and broken skeleton.

After many such spurts of speed and careful creeping, he arrived. It was bright and clear up there. A few warped cedar trees stood dangerously near, clutching at the sky. But this was part of the fun. You were no good kite-man if you could not steer your kite away from them.

The wind was harder up here — just good. Even now Ian must step gingerly over the ground, because his feet were becoming tied up in fantastic cobwebs of thread; thread tangled up beyond hope, left there by frustrated, sometimes bitterly weeping owners.

All around him there was sound. The air was humming and alive with it. Boys were in bunches sitting, standing, crouching, bending, sometimes pulling desperately at a failing kite or leaning hard away from one that was pulling stronger than a young calf.

A few of them were in raptures, looking up and calling out sweet names, groaning words of adoration for their kites were such perfect fliers that they were 'sleeping' on the wind or were 'mad bulls' humming sweetly, shifting ever so gracefully from side to side, their tails scribbling invisibly upon the blue sky. Ian's head hurt with excitement. His kite *must* fly like that.

The other kites, he hated the way they behaved. They were butting and zigging, whining like mad mosquitoes. Most of the boys who flew these mad kites were grouped together, carrying on noisily and crazily, just like their kites.

'DARBAIL!' Ian was startled. All eyes darted above the network of thread that radiated from earth to sky, to the maze of colourful kites. Ah! he saw it. There it was, sailing limply down towards earth and the green bushes. One gone! severed finally from the hands of its owner. Ian looked up. He then looked at his kite and felt unhappy. His heart was racing as though that lost kite were his own.

It was Karl's kite. He saw him leap to his feet, three friends following, spurred by the great shouts and laughter of the others. That kite may sail for miles and get stuck in the tallest of trees on the very edge of the topmost branches — impossible to retrieve. And of course the kite-raiders on the distant hills, looking and waiting patiently for just this to happen, were already on their way 'skipping' bush too. It was a question of who got the kite first. It all depended on too many things; on who got there first, where the kite got lodged and whether it was worthwhile to take it down or not. The kite was not so important, but everyone wanted thread. If raiders and owners met, a fight in the bush was a sure thing; but this was part of the fun.

Kite is fight! Ma said so. Ma also said no confusion, don't go close to the others; they always put razors on their kites. The tails were packed with razor-blades. Smart like hell too. They could cut a kite or the thread to pieces if they wanted to. He had his razor with him, in his pocket, but not for cutting other kites — just so that he could cut away the meshes of thread lying on the ground that might entangle his own kite.

Ian hesitated. To send out his kite was like exposing himself to some danger, like standing naked in the public road.

'What happen, you come to fly kite and you 'fraid to send it out?' The voice fell like a stone on his ears. He did not have to turn around: he smelled mango. Ram always smelled of old mango, in season or out of season. Ram was tall and very strong and Ian was afraid of him.

'Who say I 'fraid!'

'Well, what you waiting on?'

'I just come.'

'You lie! I see when you come.'

Ian's nostrils quivered. A warning current of danger ran through him.

'Lemme send it out for you.'

'No! I sending it out myself.'

'You want a heave?'

'Is only a flexy. Don't need no heave.'

'Is not bamboo kite alone that need heave.'

'This one light and small; no heave necessary.'

Ian prepared the kite with trembling hands. His skin was flushed and tight with the presence of Ram. He could feel Ram's dark, feverish eyes on him. Leaving the kite a few yards from him, he stepped back, thread in hand. Ram stepped forward quickly and held the kite up. All the boys were silent, eyes fixed intently on the drama before them.

'Wait!' Ian's voice was small and anguished. Ram jerked the kite upward and Ian, half-ready, struggled and gained control. He began to give the kite slack, carefully.

'Gimme a slack.'

'No!'

'Gimme a slack.'

'I say no!' The kite was going out fast, carrying the thread with it. It hummed promisingly.

'You 'fraid your thread bus'? My hand don't have garlic you know.'

'I didn't say so!'

'Ok, then.' Ram grabbed the thread, his eyes held a threat.

'Alright then, take a slack.'

'Gimme the baller.' Ram snatched the stick on which the thread was neatly wound.

'I giving it everything; I slacking down to the baller.'

'No, suppose it bus'?' Ian wanted to cry.

'Boy, move nuh. You too damn tremble.'

'Is you too bold.'

The kite began to 'sing', Ram had stopped slacking it. It stood beautifully in the wind, its tail rippling like water. It was all aglow with sun. Ian ached to hold it. But he was afraid.

He looked at the other kites with a pained yet critical eye. Some were so far out, they were mere specks up in the blue. The closer kites appeared much higher. This always puzzled him. There were all types and shapes and sizes of kites. They all had their own peculiar personalities; each of them putting the rainbow to shame for colours. Some were big and aggresive, some stylish, some just plain show-off. Others were noisy and awkward; the rest, small and cute, flitting and flying daintily like butterflies or ducking and bowing restlessly like humingbirds. But there was none like his, none at all.

A lot of them were looking at his kite. It sang sweetly above the brazen din of the others, turning and flashing majestically, every now and again, spreading both tails like a lady would her skirt, condescendingly shaking them in playful admonishment or keeping one tail straight down and curling the other up like a child scratching its head.

'Kite nice!' Ram said. He spoke quietly, and Ian, despite his anguish felt proud hearing him admit it.

'Is I make it!' Ram looked at him, something new and disturbing in his eyes. Ian felt uneasy.

'You could make another one.' It was a statement.

'Let me hold it now.'

'NO.'

'Gimme me kite.'

'Take it, nuh.'

Ian, loud and wailing; 'Gimme me kite.'

Ram angrily, 'I *not* giving you.'

'All eyes are fixed on them suspensefully.

'I goin' tell Ma.'

'Is mines now; I not giving you.'

Ian begins to tremble; his body shakes with sobs. It sounds like high pitched laughter but he is sobbing. Ram, embarrassed, begins to hate Ian spitefully, viciously for it. His foot comes down hard on Ian's knee and Ian goes berserk with the pain and the dirty hate grating through his stomach. He sinks his teeth in Ram's side. Ram shakes him off like a dog. His two hands close around Ian's head. Two hands! Ian looks up quickly, instinctively, and he sees it, his kite, sailing like a beautiful, broken bird down the sky. The silence and the blows are terrible. But his hand is out of his pocket and everything, everything and every way he feels, he does with the razor. He does not see or hear anything, not even the boys' screaming or Ram's gasping. He is sailing like a terrible kite down the hill, screaming:

'Ma . . . Maaa! O' God, Ma . . .'

The Gun

There was only the sound of their naked feet beating the asphalt road.

The man in front walked steadily on, unaware, it seemed, of the rapid pattering of smaller feet behind him. He was no more than a big, featureless form striding resolutely forward in the early morning. They had left in the wee hours when sleep was still a warm blanket over the village.

The man walked; the child followed. The light, chill air — strident with the sound of insects — rubbed itself like a cold hand against her body. Every now and then she faltered, adjusting the strap of the crocus-bag she'd been given to carry on her shoulder.

Once, when they'd passed the St. Paul's Junction, and home was miles behind, the form in front had — without pausing or breaking stride — asked in a brusque, dry voice:

'You tired?'

'No,' the answer came, in a thin, tremulous voice; no different from the tinny chittering of the crickets in the roadside grass.

The child followed the heavy footsteps in front, blind to everything else except the need to keep the rhythm — the exact pace and distance of five steps behind the man.

Now that the sky was becoming lighter, the unpleasantly stony road to the Mardi Gras mountain begun, he shortened his stride somewhat; not because of her, but because the climb was getting steeper and his breathing heavier.

'C'mon,' he grunted, leaning his body forward, the better to take the climb.

He held the gun across his front, with both hands. The muzzle was held in his left, the rest of the gun slanting downward to where he clasped the stock in his right. It was wrapped carefully in a canvas bag; done in a way to conceal the shape of the rifle from outside eyes. The child had watched him oil and polish it many times, always in the secrecy of the bedroom where only wife and sons were allowed during those hours of cleaning.

The gun was a .303 rifle furnished during the days when he was a police. He'd never used it, he said, during the Big Riot, years ago, when the police did terrible things to people. He'd never used it at the time of the Change-over when the people came to avenge their lost ones.

That was not what people said. Even Mother, when he spoke this way about himself, said nothing. She simply looked down at her feet and was silent. There was that same look on her face when, sometimes at night, he woke up in a screaming sweat and she had to hold his head and calm him.

He'd kept the gun; hidden it when the New Police came searching. And Mother said nothing because his eyes were on her and she was afraid of him because of what he would do to her if she told.

Yesterday, Mother was also afraid when he told her:

'Tomorrow, I takin' Gi-Gi wit' me.'

'Where!' Mother's eyes were frightened.

'Matti Gras. We goin' mountain-huntin. Dis is the season for monkey. Monkey-meat is the best wild meat. You dunno that?'

'But you can't take the child with you. Huntin is man' work. Why you don' take one of the boys as you accustom to!'

'The likkle girl wan' to go. She tired harrass me, man. I don' know what the hell a likkle girl wan' to be goin' huntin for. So don' ask me.'

'She can't go. You not takin' her!'

'Who goin' stop me? You!? She comin' wit' me because she ask me to. If that is the way she have to learn that huntin' is not for likkle girls then let her learn the hard way!'

'You takin' the gun?'

'Shut you' blinkin' mouth, woman! You want every-body to know my business?'

'I say, she not goin' nowhere with you!' Mother was close to tears.

'If I hear you say that again, I shove this hand right down your throat..'

Ma did shut-up because she knew he was serious.

The sun was up, her bare feet aching, as they began climbing the foothills.

The child's father skipped sure-footedly over the stones of the slippery mud-path. She stuck doggedly at his heels, her eyes fixed on his ragged, sweat-soaked, khaki shirt and his stained, rolled up trousers.

'You tired?' he asked again, turning this time, to watch her.

'No,' she fluted, her large, soft eyes brushing his hard face. 'Cruel,' she thought, remembering the word she'd learnt in school the week before: that was what teacher Claire had called the boy who bullied all his classmates! She'd kept the word in mind, remembering her father.

'Eat,' he commanded, handing her the wild guavas he snatched from the low branches. They were picking their way up a narrow ravine, thickly covered with guava trees and wild nettle. To avoid the lurking needless of the overhanging *pickah trees,* she strived to put her foot exactly where he had placed his.

He sweated profusely now, his man-smell filling her nostrils. It was neither pleasant nor unpleasant. It depended. There were times when he came home drunk and raving, and the scent of him filled her with dread. At other times when he was in a laughing mood, she was content to sit and watch him romp in the yard with her five brothers. He never played with her.

When all the houses, near and distant, had diss-appeared — swallowed up, it seemed, by the intense greenery — when there was nothing but the sound of dripping leaves and bird-noises way up in the canopy of branches, he stopped.

'Shhh,' he hissed, though she hadn't made a sound. He listened then began to unwrap the rifle.

With his bare feet, he stirred the carpet of dead leaves and revealed what might have been smooth lumps of soft, dark earth.

'Droppings,' he grunted. 'Manicou droppings. They been eating land-crabs from the ravine down there. Now if you look close, you goin' see some of the crab-shell still in dey droppings.' His demeanour was more relaxed.

The gun, now exposed, was quickly loaded with cartridges taken from the same wrapping. The child wondered for the thousandth time, her large eyes glued to the weapon, whether it was true — what had been whispered about her father.

'C'mon, girl we don' have all day.'

The child jumped; began following the man uphill.

They were soon surrounded by a small plantation of wild bananas. Bunches of fruit hung from the pendulous stems thrown out by the trees. The chill air was sweet with the scent of ripe bananas. Gi-Gi stuffed herself.

The man was exultant. The girl had never seen him so happy before. He cut a *grappe* of the largest fruits down and said it was for their return home. It was the bunches of ripe bananas that really thrilled him.

'Look at that!' he grinned. 'A lot of monkey around here. How I know that? Hah! Monkey eat ripe fig like people. They pick them off the bunch and peel them . Throw the skin on the ground like children. If was manicou dey woudda eat *into* the bunch. Look at that! If you didn' know better you woudda say it was a human-been who throw them skin on the ground. Not so?'

The child nodded.

She crept through the undergrowth behind him, her mind crowded with thoughts of the monkeys. Where were they and what did they look like? Her father had always brought them home skinned and quartered. Granny had told her once, that monkeys were caught by cutting small holes in pumpkins and placing food there. They put their hands in but could not take them out when their fists were closed around the food. Monkeys, she said, did not ever let go of the food in their hands.

They crawled through the bushes until they were looking across and downwards at the banana trees. The child stooped and listened with the man; not knowing what she was listening for. She listened until she thought she heard something. The man drew the gun from beside him, lifted it, pulled the bolt at the side back and she was sure.

It came: an increased stirring in the bushes just beyond the bananas, almost like a wind approaching, then a sudden burst of high-pitched chatter very much like children water-fighting at the stand-pipe by the road at home.

'They comin', he said, raising the gun to his shoulder and levelling it.

The child shivered, not knowing whether it was the mountain-chill or the fear beneath her anticipation.

A crowd of long-tailed, black and white creatures tumbled out of the trees. They swarmed into the banana grove and began feeding, scolding and nudging each other noisily aside. The child was ceased with shocked wonder at those white-faced creatures covered with fluffs of what appeared to be incredibily soft hair, eating bananas as she would with her bare hands. As she had eaten them not too long ago! Some of the largest animals, she noted, had young ones clinging to their backs and undersides.

The man was flat on the ground, his cheeks pressed tightly against the rifle.

The child was not prepared for the sudden thunder of the gun going off. She fell clean on her back, the forest itself seeming to capsize with her. Then she heard what must have been the animal her father had caught . . . but then, she was not sure if it were the monkey or herself that had screamed.

She sat up blinking confusedly at her father's face. What the girl saw there confirmed for her, with a certitude that belied her ten years, that all of the whisperings about him were true.

He'd lifted the gun again and Gi-Gi saw why. The monkeys had all disappeared, as suddenly as they had come. Except for one which stood in the clearing between the trees. In a moment it turned and the child realised why it hadn't run. It held a young one close against its chest, having lifted if gently off the ground. The gun was steady in her father's hand.

Then it happened: the animal turned, searched the bushes with its eyes and found them. Its gaze was direct as it lifted both arms out and up, the young one held out to them, its eyes imploring.

'Look!' the child choked, 'It sayin' — It sayin . . .'

But the man had seen. He shuddered violently, groaning the way she'd heard him groan on those nights he had his bad dreams. He dropped the gun and went careering down the hill, the little girl following as best she could.

Cold Hole

Ian stirred, his body tense with excitement.

Somebody was chopping wood on the other side of the valley. Sunlight dripped like warm butter through the holes of the old board house and settled on his naked belly.

Outside, the yard vibrated. There were the mixed smells of wood-smoke and early morning breakfast which made his nostrils quiver. The bars of sunlight made beautiful criss-cross patterns on the floor.

The birds too, were creating a racket in the trees, calling him it seemed — urging him to come out.

But in some quiet way, his senses were also strummed by subtler fingers; so subtle, one could only feel them — not speak of them. They were deep and secret things that made his body tingle, like the musty scent of damp leaves and earth-sap, the breath of trees and fruits. His feet propelled him from the floor through the open door and into the yard.

Throwing his hands high up to the sky and clouds, he toasted his face in the sun, sipped the air, and sent a shout echoing down the hill towards the river.

Dada, his great-aunt, who grand-mothered him, laughed, her voice coming through the doorway;

'That boy crazy to rarted!'

Nobody remembered, not even Kent, that today was his birthday. Thirteen years!

But the sun and the wind and the trees knew it because *they* had given him a warm day — a special day, a real birth-day-Sunday. A day for the river.

The house, though, was somehow too quiet. A quietness that Ian had learnt never to trust.

Mama was not talking, not singing; doing nothing, it

seemed. She was in a storm-cloud mood, it appeared. No one woud dare cross her path this morning. If she caught *him* — well . . . water more than flour.

Thoughts of the river came to his mind. Mama hated the river. Rather, she hated *his* going fishing.

Today, nobody and nothing was going to stop him. Not only because it was his birthday but because a bitter memory was eating his heart out — a week-old memory that was burning him up with shame.

It was an afternoon after school. Steve, Ken, his little brother, Cecil and the others were adoring him, while he rolled stories — river stories — off his tongue, polishing and colouring them with bold, vivid strokes:

> 'Cold Hole was deep and cold! I dive in!
> I dive down, down! deep-deep down, and
> guess what I see?! A big, big ling, a guage.
> Ah fuss it big, it black. It black till it rusty.
> It see me! An' it start to back-back.
> I spen' a whoole hour under water, tryin' to catch it
> so wen . . .'

'You lie!' two voices boomed behind him.

He swung around as though slapped in the face. Ashton and Mandy stood sneering above him. They cared nothing and did what they liked. It was their last year in school. Ian knew they were men, because they smelled like men.

'Who say I lie?' His voice was flecked with defiance, his cheeks burning. His friends were in a cluster, their eyes fearful.

'You dam well lie and you know you lie,' Mandy grunted at him.

Ken, flimsy and dove-like, stood at his brother's side, 'Is true. Ian ent lie!'

They laughed and the child flinched at their loudness.

'Ent lie.' Ashton's tone was pregnant with mockery. 'Who afraid of Cold Hole more than your brother here? Me an' Mandy tired lift him up to cross deep water or to climb steep river bank. I see him cry a thousan' times because he afraid of Cold Hole.'

'I no 'fraid *now!*' Ian's voice was intense.

'Since when?'

'Since I know I is *me* and not nobody shadow.'

They were all puzzled. The fierceness of his tone indicated to them that he was not playing with words.

Ashton was blunt: 'You turn foolish because you start getting fresh-up and mannish wid yourself. Little boy like you.'

Ian, turning, rested his hand lightly on his brother's shoulder, balancing on the balls of his feet. Everything had become suddenly still. Vehicles droned in the far off distance. Leaves fell and made clicking sound on the road. The suspense was terrible. Ian was crazy enough to hit one of the big boys. Even though he knew that they would murder him. Mandy's face had become stone.

'I not 'fraid,' Ian's voice trembled. He thought he was going to cry, he felt so strangely aflame. He remembered walking away from the group, head stiff, still holding his younger brother's shoulder. Even now the memory stung him.

Quickly, he disappeared beneath the house, gathered his line, his bait, an old piece of cutlass and, still bending low, crept towards the stool of banana trees fringing the house that would hide his escape. The trick was to disappear when no one was looking. When Ma . . .

'Hold it, Mister Man!' His mother's voice froze him as she carried her heavy body ever so easily over the stony yard, her large hands quickly stripping a whip from the Bowlie tree that hung over the house. How he hated that Bowlie tree!

Once, mama had caught him absorbed in trying to chop it down. She had quietly complimented him for his efforts, assuring him that the small branches would all be reserved for 'warming him up'. As for the rest of the tree, he would of course have to 'burn coals' with it.

The message sank in and left him pondering for days. The tree still flourished to punish him. Now . . .

'What day today is?' Mama's voice was almost caressing.

'Sunday, Ma.' He searched his head desperately for a

way out, 'You see, Mama, today is my birthday. You —
everybody — forget.' She paused. He sensed it. 'And I
thought that, well . . . . I go go an fish for my birthday.'

'Come!' She drew him out into the yard.

The windows of the surrounding houses suddenly
opened and spilled the upper halves of full-chested
women who, at this precise moment, decided to take a
'breeze out.' The other children were quiet. Even the
fowls ceased scratching.

'Is a naaasty habit you have! Every Sunday so, you
leaving tea behind, tying the goat any old place to starve,
and you gone and dreeve-way whole day in the river.
Suppose you drown? Suppose you drop down an' dead!'

Ma had been piling up all of his sins. Now that she had
an audience, she was exposing him for all who cared to
see, that she was a good mother — one who knew how to
bend the rod.

Her words came in torrents.

It was her war dance, her way of building up the steam
until she could contain it no longer.

'Last Sunday, I hear that Gordon cow nearly butt you
and break you likkle arse; you *so* farse. You been jookin
the man cow wid stick.'

The yard shook with laughter.

'And yesterday, you been voonging stone at Ayhie
mango tree. You nearly bus' the old lady head in she own
garden.' She shook him violently when he denied this
one. His mouth snapped shut.

'The uddah-day you tell me you goin' and help Nen
pick peas. You end up quite in the sea with Ashton and
Mandy. Which part of the sea you does pick peas eh? . . .

'And where you learn all them bad-words that you
could cuss Mr. Joe-Joe who worth you gran'faddah and
tell how he born n' where he came from; you get too dam
mannish now!'

The whip curled itself venomously around him. Pain
exploded down his back. He twisted like a mad worm.
Ma lifted him high off the ground. The children counted,
subdued, one ----- eleven . . . . Ian's scream pierced the
air when the whip fell on his back again ----- fifteen.

It was then that Dada intervened. She was old, and wrinkled like a raisin, but her voice stung like a thorn.

'Stop now, Myra. You want to spoil the blasted child skin, or what!' It checked Mama as though a hand had held her back.

Pain-crazy, Ian ripped himself loose and bolted like a mad siren through the bushes, beyond the house.

*   *   *   *   *

He sat there for a long time and fought his tears. Mama regained her voice. It rose and fell in the near distance. They had forgotten him.

Life continued.

'Ian!' Ken was calling him. He came fumbling through the *black sage* and *borbook*. As usual, he was trouser-less. Children were rarely given trousers that age to wear at home. They tore them up too quickly for their parents' meagre purse.

'I bring your fishing rod an' t'ing for you.' He was a gentle-voiced, soft-eyed child; very dusky and almost girlish in manner.

Ian snatched the things away from him, sniffing hard to control his shaking body. Ken finally handed him a rumpled paper-bag. It contained home-made bread with a big spread of guava jam. It was a generous offering — Dada's way of telling him that it was not her fault and that she cared.

'It have blood on your foot!' Ian looked at where Ken was pointing. The whip had bitten in. A string of unholy words ran through his mind. Gathering up the rod and bait, he began marching downhill through the bushes.

'I wan' come wit' you,' Ken called.

'NO!'

'I goin' carry the bait and crayfish for you.' This was usually Ken's job when they went together.

'NO!'

'I cominnn!' It was a plea, almost a cry.

'You en have no pants.'

'I custom.'

'Ants go bite you ki-kiss. And today I goin' way down by Cold Hole. It have a mermaid down there that like nice-lookin' boys wid pretty face like you.'

The truth was, he wanted to be alone. He wanted no help. It had to be as personal as possible, to prove simply that, alone, he could face this place.

Despite the zombies that lurked there, despite the dealers who met there at nights to sell children's souls to the devil, in spite of all the dark-night and shadow things that the old people told him lived in Cold Hole, he had to go. Indeed, he sometimes heard them at nights, joining the chorus of crickets and bull-frogs that sung for the moon. A distant child of a distant friend somewhere in the faded memory of Dada had gone to the river alone and disappeared. Cold Hole had taken him and was waiting to swallow anyone who choose to abandon their chores at home to go fishing.

'You can't come, Ken. I go bring a mango, piece-a-cane and a red-tail crayfish for you, kay?'

'Kay.'

Ian sniffed and smiled. He remembered half-killing a boy in school for pinching Ken. It was the only time he had fought before a teacher.

He took the mud track for the river, passing many people in their gardens. A few, he greeted with, 'Good morning.' He ignored those who usually brought complaints against him to his mother. On the way, he met Elaine, tall and big-breasted, coming up the hill with a basin of river-washed clothes balanced on her head. She was grinning wickedly. The news had already reached her.

'It damn good, yuh mudda cut yuh arse!'

'Haul you arse.' It came out with all the vehemence, the pain and humiliation of the morning's punishment. He did not even pause to look her full in the face. Elaine's loud laughter bounced down the hill behind him and did not stop until he reached the river.

*   *   *   *   *

The river took its time coming down. It began, in Ian's mind, somewhere far up among the bushes, the rain and mist of Morne Délice mountain. In many places, dazzling plots of cultivated green sloped all the way down to its very edge. On weekends he would often go to gather fire-wood on Gellineau Hill. From there he could have a good view of the valley.

Somebody had given to it its rightful name: Hope Vale. The canes stretched way down to Calivigny, smoky blue in the distance, and merged with the pastel-blue sea. The river was a dazzling thread of silver, twisting through the lap of the valley.

It was a river of many moods and rhythms. Skipping lightly over stones or simply sidestepping the 'Mako rocks,' snake-crawling through the grey silence of leafy tunnels, then suddenly leopard-leaping into day; high-flying the precipices in white abandon and finally settling in sky-blue basins that turned the sun to liquid light. The presence of the river healed the morning's pain.

This world was his world, as intimate as his most private dreams. All his fancies, vague longings, his hates and loves, were born and nurtured here among the shades of green, of filtered light and shadow. Shadows that spread out like black cloth on the banks and spilled like grey ink into the water. Every stone, every snaking root that plunged into the water were extensions of himself.

With mounting excitement, his fingers quickly baited his hook. It was simply a burnt needle, skillfully bent and attached to fine string tied to a neat and slender stick. But in his hands, it became a living thing that flipped the crayfish beating wildly out of the water. He caught them expertly and impaled them on a cleaned coconut flex. He moved steadily down river, his mind travelling ahead of him.

First he would have to pass Concrete Basin where the mullets were. They liked the deep, smoky-blue pools surrounded by big, black rocks. It was a quick hook and rapid hand that caught them. Then Dragon Place, where the water-grass and crestles made a dazzling, green carpet and the stones surfaced like heads from the water. Every species of crayfish abounded there: kakador, red-tails, swellies, and a ling or two, if one was lucky. Long Water and Young Sea were the pools where river crabs and zandomeh lived. Half mile further down was Cold Hole.

From there the river changed character. It deepened and darkened. The banks became wet and treacherous humps, riddled with crab-holes. The branches drooped low, hiding *my-bone* nests and others — creatures of his imagination that lurked in the shadows; creatures that were half-river, half-sea. Only big men went that far.

'Roses are red my love
    violets are blue,'
He whistled, to forget his forebodings.

Rosy was his sweet-heart. Rosy lived on the way from school. She did not know that Ian thought about her everyday and that in his world, they lived together, cried and laughed together. Of course he had never spoken to her in real life. She was too nice to speak to. The best of everything he had was for Rosy. Though Rosy never spoke to him and he was tongue-tied in her presence. Many of his friends', even his brothers' mouths had bled when they teased him about Rosy.

The sun was melting over the Calivigny hills, already spilling buckets of colours all over the sky when he reached Cold Hole. Four flexes bristled with crayfish. It was a proud catch. Many people working their way up-river whistled in admiration at his catch.

He had passed men 'chopping mullet.' They knelt over the pools, and with cutlasses, slashed at the fishes as they flashed past. It was a dangerous game because a cutlass swung through water became a crazy thing that flashed back at the feet of its owner.

A few others were 'shoving.' They pushed their bare hands under stones, dragging out by force any living thing. It was a daring sport also. If they were lucky, they would pull out a 'ling' or a young guage. This was a lobster-sized crayfish, zebra-striped and awesome, that clung murderously to their fingers. Most of the time, their hands came out with river-crabs, water snakes or bull-frogs.

It was good fun watching the way the shover's expression would change from joyful excitement to violent disgust.

There were lots of thick-fleshed women labouring and laughing over multi-coloured mounds of clothes. They often talked to him or teased him as he passed along. In return, he threw them sun-yellow guavas and water-lemons collected along the river banks. A mango or two, if he knew them well.

The sapodillas and sugar-apples were hidden in his shirt. The *gru-grus* also, were for sale in school the next day. His mouth was white, his tummy tight, from sugar cane. No one could go hungry in the river. Not even if one wanted to.

*   *   *   *   *

He arrived, tired but intoxicated with the long walk, the endless bird noises and insect sounds. Already, he began to feel the chilliness — the sinister nature of the place. No wonder people talked so many times against coming here.

It was a very deep basin, roofed by thick-hanging vines and interlocked leaves and branches. Light filtered through like transparent smoke. A direct ray of sun never touched these waters. Here, everything was hushed. A wall of moss-covered rock plunged down and buried its feet in the darkness of the basin.

The water was so dark, so lifeless, it was as though he was looking into a gaping hole.

Ian knelt down and rested his things on the bank, recognising in the gloom an overturned calabash with a heap of rice around it. His heart leapt. Ian knew for a fact that this was the meeting place of Saraka people. Those who drank the blood of fowls and dealt in the affairs of spirits; they spoke to them in a strange language and came here to offer rice and saltless food to Orisha — goddess of the waters. A chill snaked through him.

His eyes focused on the pool. He had to move fast. It would be dark within the hour. Then it would be impossible to fulfill his resolve. Somewhere there beneath the waters, was a hole in the rocks. It was a place where Ashton never failed to catch a *guage*. They were the biggest of the biggest crayfishes. So old, they were rusted at the limbs and back from head to tail. Too strong for any hook, their teeth shone white and distinct on their pincers.

Standing at the brink of the void, the grey quietness stirred an acute sense of loneliness in him. Ian signed himself the way Dada had taught him to, and stripped himself naked, feverishly wrapping his crayfishes with his clothes so that lizards could not get at them.

He stood at the water's edge, so still, that for a moment he appeared like a clay statue. He summoned all his courage and plunged. The sudden cold shocked his body, penetrating him like needles. He swam exactly as Ashton did, stretched forth his hand at the precise place and moment and surfaced against the rock-wall. The water folded over him as he allowed himself to sink like a stone. He closed his eyes, felt for the hole, discovered the sudden break in the rock, and sent his hand in. Soft mud yielded beneath his groping fingers, oozed through and around them and stirred suddenly like a living thing.

Something dark and long and slippery flashed out; passed like a cold hand across his nakedness. The water churned and he was up in a wink — threshing desperately for the bank.

It was back on the bank that he realised what it was. A river-eel, a zangri! His body shook like a leaf though he felt somehow embarrassed. Fear had literally chased him out of the water. It had made a mockery of him. He hated fear!

He knelt on the bank until his body dried. He was no longer trembling. Something had begun to stir in his heart while his eyes measured the water, the bank, the rock-wall. This time it was not fear that made his heart pump the blood in giddying spurts up his head.

Again at the edge of the pool he tensed, arched his

body like a bow and plunged. His body sliced the water and disappeared. Again its coldness seized him. Rapidly, he made for the hole. Still down, it was impossible to see the bottom of the pool. He surfaced quickly, packed his lungs and dived again. He sank himself and reached the gap again, easing his hand in. The jaggedness of the hole surprised his fingers. It went deep, up to the shoulders. When he could send his hand no farther, he felt the whiskers of the guage. It sent a tremor through his spine. Something hard and sharp suddenly grated against the palm of his hand. He withdrew rapidly and surfaced, snorting water and gulping in air. His heart was racing. Determination and excitement spurring him, he went down again, pushing his hands forcefully in, fingers closing rapidly. Pain instantly shot through his arm as though somebody had driven nails through him. The water stifled his cry. He began to pull.

The muscles of his back and stomach tightened until they hurt.

It was like ripping a piece of rock away. His head darkened and hollowed. It was impossible to hold out any longer.

As a child, he was accustomed to uprooting manioc trees from the earth. Work that only men of the village should do, Dada used to warn him. All these muscles came to play, protesting against the terrible strain. Just when he was about to give up and surface for sheer need of air, he felt the guage slip. Inch by inch it came. Resisting. Finally it came out. Fighting.

Ian catapulted to the surface and struck for the bank in a confusion of water. Held, struggled, slipped and finally heaved himself on the bank.

He half-lay, half-knelt on the wet leaves and mud and watched the crayfish clinging to his hand, dripping blood and water. It was enormous. Its crablike eyes stood out of the slots. The powerful tail was spread out like a fan, beating the air. Slowly, painstakingly, he broke off the pincers buried in his wrist. His hands still throbbing from the pain, he watched the guage for a long time while it convulsed defiantly on the wet ground. He watched it for an infinite length of time. And slowly, the memories came back to him — Ashton and Mandy, Mama and the morning's whipping.

Four bright red spots remained where he had been pierced. Strange emotions stirred in him, things he had never felt before. Rosy, home, Dada — everything — went far, far away and did not matter. After all, he did not care for anyone to know. He had done what a lot of people, even men, real men would never dare try. He would do even more than Ashton and Mandy. And they would never know. It would remain his secret; his victory. Slowly and almost dreamlike, he rose, hung his heel over the head of the crayfish and in the timeless gloom, crushed its head into the wet earth.

Ian looked around, eyes bright, body tense as though seeing the place for the first time and, with a clear shrill voice, he shouted loud and long down the long, gaping river-corridor; down through the sunless silence and shade, hanging thickly over the rest of the river; his voice defying the cold, impersonal death-stillness of the pool.

He turned, suddenly, triumphantly, taking up his things, and ran through the shade into the fading day. The remaining light fell and draped itself around his small body. His footprints remained deeply and clearly etched on the dark bank behind him. He headed for home.

Dark Is The Hour

The child raised his head when he heard the door scrape. 'Daddy!' he thought. His heart leapt with a relief that surprised him. His head sank back slowly toward the floor and his heart was heavy.

'Gertrude,' his father's voice was low, gruff.

The boy didn't answer. He peeped under his arm at his father's dark shape leaning against the door. A bundle was in his right hand and in his left he balanced his cutlass. The child's eyes leapt open wide, his breath catching in his throat. Slowly, his father's shape doubled and he saw him quietly place the bundle and cutlass in the corner near the door.

'Gerty!' his father repeated. His voice was still low; drained it seemed — drained and hope-wearied. The child on the floor was aware of his father's deep pause, his meditative silence. He pressed his face deep in the bedding until the floor was hard against his cheek, fighting the tremors in his body, tightly bunching his toes. He felt the weight of his father's heavy boots sinking in the floor-boards as he stepped cautiously over the little girl, then the younger boy and finally, himself on the floor.

The room, already half-dark, darkened further as the man's shadow fell across the floor onto him. The boy saw him reach for the tiny kerosene lamp on the table and turn it up.

Without turning, the boy knew that this father was staring at the bed in the corner, against the wall. He waited, fearing the wrath that could follow that pause. He knew his father would find just the bed, dirty as usual, rumpled and empty.

It was unbearable, the suspense and silence, the tense waiting for his father's next move. The boy could even hear the man's breathing from where he stood, coming low and deep. He lay there waiting, expecting . . .

His small body bunched suddenly and involuntarily as the heavy weight of his father's hand dropped on his thin back, shaking him in a rough-gentle manner. It was meant to awaken him. His father thought he was asleep, and from fear, he pretended sleep, going through all the motions of someone just awakened.

Even while the man shook him, his voice was repeating, insisting, 'Stanford! Fordy, wake up boy. Stan boy! Where you' modder? Wake up. Tell me, whe' you modder is?'

And when the boy sat up and opened his eyes, it was to stare directly into his father's, close to his, tense and urgent, fearful and expectant.

The boy shifted hs face away, slightly. He fixed his eyes on the paper-pasted board walls across the room. Through the deep night he heard sounds: the insidious drone of vehicles and sometimes louder and sharper noises. A deeper fear seized him. For it was night, and outside the flimsy house he knew the darkness threatened.

'I talking to you, boy! This time, there was no mistaking the way his father shook him. He detected the unmistakable edge of anger in his tone.

'Sh' . . . Sh' . . . She gone!' the boy answered, and the pain of the day and the night began to show on his small face. His father's eyes followed the drops trickling down his face, pausing at his cheek, then slipping onto his own dirty shirt. Half-consciously, he reached out his hand to brush the drops from the boy's face. The boy flinched involuntarily.

'Hush!' the man said, quietly, in his rough-gentle manner. His hands fell limply back against his sides.

'When she gone? She say where she going? She leave any message? Who . . . What she went wid? She leave any message?'

The questions came in a flood. The man didn't wait

for an answer; didn't seem to expect any. His voice was a strange combination of listlessness and urgency and impotent desperation. His face tightened, came slack again alternately.

The little girl woke up crying. The boy turned to her quickly; automatically began patting her back gently and cooing softly, sending her back to sleep. The man was fascinated, seeing this as if for the first time.

He left the boy suddenly, the lamp still held in one hand, and knelt low to the floor. He began to feel under the bed. A basin rattled harshly against something hard. He did not appear to want to stop searching. With wide eyes the boy watched him stretching his hand far up under the bed, feeling, fumbling, still feeling. His movements were frantic; on his face was a quiet desperation.

Finally he stood up with a great, lingering effort. In the yellow lamplight, his face glistened with sweat.

'She gone,' he muttered thickly. The words tumbled out of his mouth, empty and meaningless, wrung dry, it seemed; as though the realisation had just struck him. 'De *grip*', she take dat too. She gone. You' modder gone for good.' His eyes were dark and unbelieving.

The little girl had got up again she was crying in loud, sharp spurts. The boy lifted her onto his lap. He began to rock her and hum in a low, monotonous drone:

Hush Po' Po' Hush
Mammy gone to town . . .'

His father stopped him. 'When last you feed she?'

The boy pointed at the 'baby-bottle' on the table. It was an ordinary beer bottle with a rubber nipple over the mouth.

'Dis ev'ning. I make sweet-water fo' she. Milk done yestiday.' Unconsciously he spoke in his mother's clip-ed phrases.

'And you, all you' eat?'

'Steve did crying fo' hungry. I boil de las' fig da' was there. I leave some fo' you.'

The little girl had fallen asleep again. He blurted out, his face twitching, trying hard not to cry:

'Mammy, she leave since morning, just after you . . . you . . .' His voice trailed off in tears. He was shaking when he said, 'She send me by Nen-Nen . . . for . . . to borrow salt an' when I come back, she gone.'

His father turned, began to stray around the room aimlessly, passing his hands over the walls, the table in a strangely ghost-like manner. He rested over the bed, staring and muttering distractedly.

'De bed,' he said, 'didn't even make up the bed. Not even the bed.'

Words began to flow from him in a low and long lament, a listless chant that rose and fell hollowly, heavily upon the baffled ears of the boy.

'Is how I mus' feel? Not cold I mus' feel? Is me who cause crisis? Me who en't want to give wuk? Is not cold I mus' feel? Is nothing I could do. She know is not'ing I could do. Is the same drown I drowning that everybody drowning. Now she leave you in me han' fo' what? What I mus' do? Is not col' I mus' feel?'

He left the bed and trailed aimlessly around until he stood over the bundle in the corner. He removed the cutlass carefully and took up the bundle, opening it as he seated himself in the doorway.

'Look!' he told the boy. 'I bring somet'ing. I GET somet'ing; I wasn't idling. I GET somet'ing.'

He began to lay an assortment of articles on the floor. The boy saw a jumble of what looked like yams and potatoes and a few other unrecognised heaps. 'Look, these ripe, full yuh belly..'

The father handed him two large ripe bananas. The boy took them. They were wet and he wiped them on his 'nightie'. He dropped them when he saw the blood.

'Is all right,' his father said. 'De blood come from the fowl.' He indicated two placid heaps on the floor. 'Is better when dey dead, easier to carry, no noise.'

He took up the bananas, wiped them on his own shirt and gave them to the boy. He took them, fixing his eyes uncertainly on the sleeping children.

'Let dem sleep. It have more, in the morning,' said his father.

The man turned away from the child and settled himself in the doorway. The boy was quietly eating behind him. The thought kept turning in his head. She didn't have to go, no reason to go — to leave him alone with the children. They fought almost every day now, it was true. But she didn't have to leave him. He hadn't believed her when she said she would leave him one of these days. He was expecting her to cook the food he had brought tonight. It would have been nice if she had stayed and cooked the food and given the children a good feed. He had been thinking about it all the way home.

He raised his head heavily. The night was pressing close and breathing ominously around him, forcing its presence through his thoughts. He heard Rovers growling away in St. George's Town below and the far sounds of lone dogs howling, lost in the dark depths of the night before him. Everything was brooding, suspended, punctuated by occasional shots that accentuated the heavy stillness. And the wind snoring through the thick bamboo clump that hung over the tiny house was a strangely disturbing dirge to his ears. He raised his slow eyes to the finger-like, fluttering leaves groping darkly, sightlessly at the night sky.

The child yawned. The man stirred; turned towards him. The last banana skin, licked clean, was drooping limply between his small fingers. The man watched him and remembered the way he had sent the little girl to sleep, the somehow striking seriousness of his quaint, little maternal ministrations. He was small for his eleven years. Standing there in the corner, naked except for his 'nightie' (one of his father's very old shirts), his frailty was painfully evident.

The man also remembered that the child had told him that he had boiled figs and left some for him. He noticed that the boy was watching him too, swaying slightly on his thin feet.

'Come . . . Look, mo' fig. You wan' mo' fig?' The boy shook his head, timidly. 'No? You wan' sleep den? Come an' sleep.' The boy approached, the lamplight exposing his naked front.

'You wan' sleep, eh Stan Fe?' The man's voice was low. The boy's eyes were deep and expressionless. There was something new in his father's voice, a deep kind of recognition played on his face.

'Come *do'do'* on me. Res' you'self. Lemme put you to sleep.' He lifted the boy, passing his hands lightly over his body, and rested him easily in his lap. The boy lay in a little heap. He turned his sleepy eyes shyly on the man's face. His mouth creased into a tiny smile before his eyes drooped and closed. He didn't hear his father crying. He was asleep.

Song For Simone

Every morning the town was awakened by the soft bleating of a sole trumpet and the light melodies of a piano. At exactly quarter to five, for the past fifty years, Beethoven's *Minuet in G* would come wafting down from the hill above St. George's and, like a fuzzy white hand, prise off the warm coverlet of sleep.

The music would pass; not abruptly, but ever so lightly, like bubbles on the wind; so that the silence too, became part of the melody.

It was always the same: the melody, then the silence that was music too. After, the cathedral's clock on Church Street — massive, masculine, sonorous — struck the hour: BONG! one; BONG! two . . . . five strokes!

Like all the mornings before, Simone stirred and stretched her long legs over the arm of the settee in the small hall where her mother had relegated her with the muttered excuse that she was a big girl now and the bedroom had become too small for both of them.

The girl opened large, attentive eyes and listened. Sure enough, there came the rumble of Togo the Dustman's cart, trundling down her street. The Dustman, they called him — the funny old man who foraged among the bins so early before the trucks came to take the refuse away. The humble thunder of his wheels was fading down the street just as the trucks arrived with their usual bang and clatter.

Soon there would be cars whooshing past; doors banging in subdued haste; feet shuffling in the rooms, partitions apart. And on the Carenage below, the watchman's whistle would come, sharp like a stricken bird, releasing the stevedores from their night shift.

Nita, her mother, came out and switched on the naked light-bulb that shared its light with the two rooms. Still heavy with sleep, she stretched, yawning furiously, as though angry at the lethargy of her limbs. There was a stirring in the bedroom, a grunt, the bed protesting noisily, then the scraping of feet on the concrete floor.

The girl did not like her mother's new man-friend. She'd decided that the moment he'd crossed the threshold the night before. But then, she never liked any of them; even though she always voiced approval whenever her mother asked.

'Come on, Sim! Get up, girl.'

But Simone had already anticipated the order. With a smooth, deft movement of her body, she was on her feet. Such agility never ceased to amaze Nita.

Sim was as tall as she, slim as a whip and still growing. Nothing disturbed Nita more than her daughter's height and what she called her 'strong complexion' which were somehow unaccountable. Moreso, because Sim's father was a regular-sized, brown-skinned man and she, as anyone could see, was not so dark or tall.

'Well,' she would conclude, 'it must have been de weather o' something.'

The girl could never understand her mother's last remark, uttered, it seemed, in all seriousness.

She busied herself with the small kerosene stove on the table near the settee, hearing, but not listening to Nita's girlish voice — a tone Simone had learnt to associate with the presence of a man-friend.

Simone worked silently and swiftly, kneading the flour, breaking and rolling the dough into small balls, then flattening each one before placing it in the frying pan of sizzling oil.

'No eggs dis mornin', she noted mentally,' so, is de usual dry bakes an' milk. Good for de man. Bad fo' me. Not so good fo' me modder.'

The church clock boomed the half hour. Nita came out dressed for work, the man trailing behind. He eyed the girl sheepishly. She had that effect on people. She remembered her mother telling her once, that her friend — it was Peter then — used to complain that Sim made him uneasy with those big, dark eyes looking right into his head. Well, they *were* looking into his head. After all, he proved to be a scamp — a married one, at that.

Nita bit the food resentfully, as though hating the idea of finishing and leaving for work.

Strange how her mother's fears grew, even as Sim grew; warning her always of the same thing, pounding it in till the words echoed in her head. First, it was to stay clear of boys; now it was men she had to beware of. Nita no longer introduced her men-friends either. They came, stayed awhile — some longer than others — then dissapeared.

Only once did the man look at her — a frank, curious stare. The girl knew the fierceness with which her mother would attack him if she suspected the slightest advance in that look. A frowning, serious man, the girl thought. He chewed the food as though he was thinking with his jaw. At least, the others used to smile.

'You know anythin' bout music?' Simone asked, staring directly at him. She was surprised at her own question, not even knowing the man's name. Besides, she'd promised her mother she was never going to ask that very question to any more of her men-friends. Strangely, Nita said nothing. She was smiling.

The man took a long time swallowing. He swilled his tongue around his mouth, passed his hand across his lips as if it were most important that his mouth be clean before the words come out.

'You call Steelpan-music, music?'

Simone frowned, considering; 'Well . . . erm — why not?'

'No-no-no! I want a straight answer. Yes or no?' He placed the rest of his breakfast on the table and rested both elbows on the rough surface. The fingers of each hand were clasped together in a curiously comic, yet dignified posture.

'Yes,' the girl answered, somewhat irritably, 'is music, oui.'

'Then,' the man said, 'I'z boss musician! I know a lot about it.'

Simone watched them leave.

Before plunging into the noise of rushing cars and
work-hurrying feet in the street below, Nita turned, and
fixing the girl with solemn eyes, delivered one of her
parting sermons.

'James leave some change on de table. Buy some
foodstuff when you come from school. One dollar is
yours fo' lunch. An' make sure none o' dem likkle boys or
nobody interfere wid you o' follow you from school. Don'
cook nothing'; I goin' see what I scrape up by de Ole
Birds. C'mon James!' And with that, they were gone.

Scrape up! That was Nita's most beaten expression.
She scraped to make a living, to pay the rent, to send
Sim to the Anglican school on Church Street. She
bowed and scraped, she said, to keep her job as a
domestic with Mr. and Mrs. McWiggin — the old couple
who lived in the big cream house on the hill that stood
above them.

It was from that house the music came each morning
to insert itself into the town's half-sleep. Simone gri-
maced resentfully at the thought of the McWiggins and
their house on the hill.

To escape the rush and squabble of the tenants from
the neighbouring rooms, the girl hastened to the shower
outside — a long stem of pipe standing in a small
enclosure of corrugated iron sheets. She stripped herself quickly and let the cold water fall on her, scrubbing
herself with long luxurious strokes, wary at the same
time, of the eyes that might be fixed on her from the
windows of the small dwellings crowding the alleyway.

There were so many things Nita didn't know about
her. True, she wanted to hear everything that took place
at school and, wherever the girl might want to go, Nita
made it her duty to accompany her. Else, Simone would
be made to remain home bored with her mother's
constant nattering.

Even whilst acknowledging the silliness of the conviction, Simone couldn't help feeling that in some way,
her mother's growing estrangement was connected with
the music from the hill. It was a misgiving that had the

strength of fact in her mind.

The month before, she remembered telling her about that startling change in her body's chemistry. Nita did not react the way the girls at school said *their* mothers did. No. Her mother came close to tears. She spoke so strangely too!

'Don't want you to do like me, Sim,' she said. 'Do me anythin' and I goin' take it, long as you give you'self time to become woman. Sometimes I wish you never grow up. Be glad to take care o' you for the rest of me life. When I was fourteen, I had you. I don' regret, but it spoil me chances. If you was a boy I wouldn't mind so much.' Then Nita had kissed her and, without really understanding why, she too was sad with her mother's sadness.

If she was a boy! How many frustrating, profoundly angering times had she heard that?

Simone hummed while she washed. She knew every note, every nuance of the morning melody. Something was lacking in that music. She did not know what it was. But every day for the past year, she found herself fighting to define it. The struggle had often thrown her into silences so deep, they despaired Nita who thought it was some strange illness that had overcome her daughter. A sense of yearning it was; of craving even, like those hungry times when she used to go to bed on an empty stomach and dream of food — blissful, warming food.

In the midst of filling herself, she would sometimes be awakened and would lay back cursing, feeling abjectly deprived, as though the meal was real and had in truth been snatched away.

During the Carnival, the year before, it was terrible. The trumpet and piano played all day, clashing with the dance and chant of the streets below. Like shattered glass, the music fell — sharp, obtrusive, admonishing. She slept fitfully that night, hating herself, even in sleep. She'd dreamt of trumpets and pianos, ranged derisively on Market Hill, pitched in triumphant battle against the steel drums and gaudily dressed calypsoes of Carnival.

'Nita!' she'd begged, 'ask dem people you work for, what is de name o' dat music they play every mornin?'

She knew now that it was called Minuet, composed by someone who lived long, long ago in a country far, far away.

'High class music,' Nita said proudly, as if the fact of working in the kitchen of old Mr. and Mrs. McWiggin made her high class too.

'Is real music,' Simone was informed. 'Classic music o' something. De ole Birds been playin' dat music fo' the past sempty years. Dem fadder an' gran'fadder play it when them was alive. You see dey uses to be gentry once — own a lot o' land and servants. Now dem have only dat big house and what their son sen' dem every mont' from Englan' — jus' enough to keep their nose pointin' up. De ole lady always talk about old times as if she regret. Say dat she is from pure Irish stock — white folks. But somewhere along the line a little nigger-blood creep in. You can't tell she dat though! She'll kill you. De only blood she want to hear about is Irish. Like it have a diff'rent colour o somethin'. Irish! Is de place where all dem white potato come from, you know.'

'Don like no Irish potato,' Simone muttered, sourly.

'Is why you eat it so greedy,' retorted her mother.

Nita talked about the McWiggins each evening when she returned home. Fortnights, she cursed the meagre sum she received for washing them, feeding them and cleaning for them. More often, she blessed them for the food she was sometimes allowed to take home.

In recent months she had begun to worry because the old man was going blind — and dotish too, she suspected — and the old lady's legs were failing her.

'Dunno how I goin' manage if I lose dem,' she would moan before lapsing into frowning silence. She thought that perhaps their son would return from overseas to run the house. That meant she might still have the job.

In all the years of her mother's working for the old couple, Simone had never seen them. Yet she felt she knew their faces, wrinkled like white raisins; their nagging tremulous voices, calling — always calling:

'*Nita!*' to lift them, lead them, clean them . . . .

There was a name for it — this leaflike paling and quailed falling. If only she could remember that sentence she had underlined the day before in her reading book! A word that had the same deliberate ring of the bell-tower on Church Street, chiming in the evening half-dark. Ah-hah! That was it. *Decline. That* was it!

Simone left for school, the chiming of the bell-tower going over and over in her mind.

Nita warmed the meal of chicken, rice and mixed vegetables she had brought from work. One of the usual power failures had thrown the town in darkness, giving the night outside a certain closeness that Simone liked. People talked. Cars passed. The night breathed.

The dirty light of the sputtering stove threw large, dancing shadows across the room. Her mother was silent — unusually so — for a long while. Simone unwound her length till her legs jutted over the settee. She waited, her large eyes luminiscent in the dim room.

'You like 'im?' Nita asked, without turning to look at her.

'Who?' The girl knew, but thought she should still ask.

'Him, erm, James.'

'No Don' think so.'

Nita turned. 'Why. You never say dat befo' with . . .'

'Them others?' Her mother had sounded hurt.

'Yes! You always like dem.'

'Dey was diff'rent.'

'Why?' Nita queried

'Dunno.'

'You goin' like 'im, Sim. He really, really nice. I know 'im long time. Jus' didn' have time fo' 'im, you know. He jus' sort o' serious; dat's all. Used to be a school teacher, and you know what school teacher' face look like.'

'What work he doin' now?'

'Work wit' de gov'ment, I think.'

'Doin' what?'

'Uhm'. Nita's face was a mixture of anxiety and confusion.

'You not tellin' me?'

'Yeh, man! Is music he teachin'.' Her mother would have left it at that, but the girl was relentless.

'What kind o' music?'

'All kind.'

'Pan-music, not so?'

'Somethin' so.'

'So why you 'fraid to say so?'

'You say you don' like 'im.'

'It don' have nothin' to do with that.'

'He comin' later.' Nitas eyes were pleading for the girl's acceptance.

'Let 'im come then.'

They ate, observing each other in silence. Nita sulked over the food. Simone, expressionless, chewed slowly and with obvious pleasure.

'Is nice food,' she purred, a small conciliatory smile suffusing her face. Then the girl extended her arm and traced long, loving fingers down her mother's face, pausing briefly at her chin. Nita smiled back a child's smile.

'Wash the wares,' she yawned, and went in.

Mr. James visited regularly. The McWiggins declined slowly. Nita worried increasingly. The leaves had quailed even more now and Simone began to wonder when they were going to touch ground.

Sometimes, the girl listened to her mother and the man talking long into the night. They laughed a lot together. Their laughter even woke her on mornings just before the minuet came sneaking down the hill to play on her mind for the rest of the day.

Early one morning Mr. James got up to work on something he called his 'new arrangement.' He came out and sat on the only chair in the hall. Simone observed him, through narrowed eyes, poring over a jumble of lines and scratches on a sheet of paper. Occasionally, he would hum, scratch the paper with his pencil, tap his feet rapidly then mutter angrily and scratch again. She recognised the tune. It was a stirring calypso named Busy Body, composed by one of the local calypsonians.

He stopped when the minuet started, cocking his ears and leaning his body toward the music that came faintly raining down on them.

'Ludwig Van Beethoven,' he breathed. 'Minuet in G! 'G' as in Jeezan Christ. What, man! You travel dam' far, oui! Not bad. Not bad at all. It have some conviction there. But it come from de *head* man! Not de heart!'

Simone's eyes shot wide open. She sat up abruptly, unaware that she had startled the man who was speaking mockingly to himself.

'Yeh, dat's it. You notice too? Somethin' missin, not so?'

'What missin'?' Mr. James seemed interested. He was taking her seriously.

'Dunno,' the girl answered, throwing herself back. 'Dunno. Just a feelin'; dat's all.'

'Explain it, then!'

Simone felt suddenly shy. She had never revealed her secrets to anyone before. They would have thought she was crazy anyway! Besides, how did a person explain that something was missing from what he or she knew nothing about?

'Well,' she said finally, 'to me — you see, is like food — nice food. You eat and eat as much as you want, but it not heavy. It never fill you up solid-like. In de end you still left empty, hungry. De sauce there but the dumplin' missin', sort of.'

Mr. James grinned, 'Dat's a nice way o' puttin' it.'

'You know what missin' then?' she asked, hopefully.

'Is not for me to say, Miss. Is for you to find out. You want to find out?'

'How?' she asked, with something like hostility in her voice.

Nita had by then come out and was standing at the bedroom's entrance regarding them closely.

'Well, perhaps if you learn to play music—pan, I mean — you'll understand what buggin' you. You talk like a person who have music in dem. Dunno, you ever hear 'bout Calinagoes? Is my band; I arrange the music. It goin' be hard 'cause the band-leader don' like girl-players. I could try to bust through hi' ignorance. You couldn' say what you said if you didn' have music in you.'

Simone was flattered, 'You think so?'

'No!' Nita said, flatly.

'No what?' asked Mr. James.

'Sim don' have time fo' dat. I don' want her mixin' wit' all dem ramgoats who does play steel band.'

'So I'z a ramgoat now! I does play steel band.'

'I didn' say dat.'

'I could find a lotta name to call people like you who does call us ramgoat. So you'z one o' dem too!' Mr. James was fuming

'All I sayin' is she not playin.'

'Why you don' let 'er decide for sheself?'

'Who the hell is you to tell me what my child must and mustn't decide? I say, no! And it goin' stay, no!' Nita's voice could be heard five rooms away.

Mr. James didn't answer but his eyes were eloquent with the effect of the insult.

Simone was to later learn that the man's temper could be as scathing as her mother's. But he preferred to conduct his battle outside of the girls presence. Unlike Nita, his voice never rose above the confines of the tiny bedroom. Though she could hear his low rumble rising and falling like the waves on the Carenage during periods of bad weather.

She followed the arguments more by her mother's indignant responses to Mr. James' remarks. What did he mean by giving the girl 'a chance to find sheself?' snorted Nita at his 'chupid' talk. How could he say she was afraid? Afraid of what? She wanted to know. It was alright for him to say that she wasn' helpin' the girl by tyin' her down because *he* didn' have no child to worry about. He had no right to ask her if she knew what Sim might be feelin' 'bout all this. What! By limitin' the girl she was limitin' herself too? What did he know? — this sonova . . .

Nita must have struck him then because Simone heard the sharp thack! of flesh on flesh, then a pro-longed scuffling that ended abruptly in silence.

This hateful man! Unasked, he'd put her feelings so
well, dissipating thus, the basis of a confrontation she
expected — in fact looked forward to — someday with
Nita. So many of her friends — the bigger girls in school
— had told her of *their* struggles with their parents.
She'd come to believe that it was part of growing up, in
the same way the fleshing out of her body was. In killing
that possibility, wasn't the man depriving her of something?

Nita threw him out the next day, then became
miserable in a way Simone had never seen before. She
ate little, went to bed early and no longer complained
about her Old Birds on the hill. There wasn't any new
menfriends either.

The seventh week having passed, Simone felt unable
to bear the gloom that stood like an ugly wall between
them. She asked, cautiously, 'He goin' come back?'

'You want 'im to come back?'

'Me? Nah, well, is up to you.'

'No-no-no, is not up to me! You think I should . . . .'

'Sort of — is up to you, Nita.'

'Is *not* up to me!!' the woman burst out. It was not
anger, but embarrassment that flared her nostrils and
sent her eyes shifting wildly from side to side.

'Is not up to me!' she repeated. 'You — I want *you* to
tell me to talk to 'im.'

'Well, tell 'im then.'

For the first time in seven weeks Nita relaxed and
really smiled. She seemed slightly ashamed of herself.

'I never see a person selfish like you,' she said light-
heartedly. 'Leaving everything up to me. No mercy!
Dat's wot! You talk like big woman who dunno how to
advise people. No heart! I goin' sorry fo' you husband.'

Husband! Simone thought, contemptuously. Don't
want no husband. Not if they made a person so soft and
stupid and crazy at the same time. Spoilin' a person'
appetite fo' everything — like this Mr. James had done
her mother. Mebbe that was the point of growin' up? —
of maturing? — to become all softee and weaky and cry-
cry, like a baby! She couldn't see the sense in it.

Nita was chattering happily away:

'He say he goin' come back on one condition. I have to
give you likkle mo' freedom — you should play pan if you
want to, and explo' the world. Crazy talk if you ask me,
because I never hold you back from explodin' de worl',
does I?'

Simone ignored the question. She asked with frowning realisation, 'So you *does* see 'im?'

'Not really. I call 'im once-or-twice on de Ole Bird
phone. Mos' time he not in office. He never does call me
back.' She sounded annoyed.

'You ask 'im to come back arready?'

'What chupidness you askin me? I never answer no
chupid-girl question!'

Simone stared at the light-bulb, smiling.

Mr. James returned and the two were laughing and
arguing as though nothing had ever happened. Simone
could not intimidate him with her stare. Her effort was
made more difficult by Mr. James' telling Nita that her
daughter had what he called classic Afro features.

'Beautiful,' he added. 'Something that your Old
Birds' failing eyesight will pass right over.'

The man did not take Simone to join his band. He
insisted that he teach her the 'basics' first and that Nita
sit with them while he talked about steeldrums — how
and why they were made

Mr. James spoke with great deliberation leaving
images in their heads of fire, gang wars, police, steel and
blood. He spoke as of a birth that spanned not months,
but decades.

'In other words,' he concluded, 'whenever you hear
the sweet notes from a steelpan, you hearin' love and
violence turn music. The violence aint finish yet; nor the
love. But is more love now, and it just start.'

He then threw his challenge at Simone, one that filled
her with doubt, anger and a profound sense of betrayal.
Yet her anger was not directed at him or anyone in
particular.

'Girls' Mr. James said, 'now playin' in quite a few
bands. Was not easy to get them in. But it happen' slow

and sure. *That* was the beginning of a new type of warfare! The fellas resist at first. Them come to the battle wit' every argument possible. Was not easy, I tell you!'

Calinagoes was his band; he arranged for them; played with them. He tried everything to get girls in; but Moose, the band's leader, would not have it. No way, Sir! This time however, he'd made some progress. They were recruiting new players for the Carnival which was three months away and he'd proposed Simone. There was a problem, though. He'd told Moose that the girl he was proposing was a good player, had already played in a band; was, in fact, the best tenor player this side of St. George's! She could even teach *them* a thing or two about music. He would bring her along in six weeks' time.

Nita's indignation crashed down like the roof on the man's head. She cursed him until she was out of breath. He waited patiently until she had burnt herself out. Then, as if explaining to Simone, he said, dryly:

'Your mother have a temper. One day it goin' fly up right up to she head and kill she. Pay attention, girl 'cause I have just six weeks to make you the best tenor panist this side o' St. George's.'

From then on the man taught Simone with a passion matched only by his firmness. She recited chords: majors, minors, sharps, flats, sevenths, ninths. He spoke confusingly of melody, phrase, tempo, timing and attack till her head became a hive of jumbled symbols and definitions.

They were gruelling — these sessions; yielding no pleasure, making her feeling of being caged in even more acute. Yet the sense of challenge did not leave her. She fought stubbornly, until gradually, beats began to take their places within bars, notes within phrases, phrases within melody; until the minuet from the hill could be listened to, stripped naked, dismantled and thrown aside until the following morning.

Mr. James betrayed little satisfaction with her progress.

'Now,' he breathed, as though only just beginning. 'Take a look at this, Af.' He'd started calling her Af for reasons which she could not understand and would certainly have resented anyway if she knew.

Before her, he placed a broad sheet of bristol-board on which was painted a large, carefully drawn tenor pan.

A work of art it was. The sides were coated in silver paint, and like the real thing, the face of the instrument bellied inward. The notes, etched out in stark relief, tapered downward with the contours of the pan.

The man handed her two rubber-tipped sticks and ordered her to strike the notes. Nita giggled and the girl became numb with embarrassment.

'Shoosh!' It was the first time he'd ever raised his voice so loud. Nita sulked back into herself. 'Go ahead, Af.'

'Is a waste o' time,' Simone said, putting as much sting as she could muster in her voice.

'Gimme the sticks!' Mr. James snatched the sticks from her and began tapping the notes, imitating with his voice, the sound of a tenor pan — a different tone to every one of the numerous notes he touched.

The girl laughed then. He seemed so intent on what he was doing. As far as he was concerned, it was the real thing. Nita's burst of laughter joined the girl's. Mr. James looked up, creased his forehead a moment and began laughing too. He suddenly declared he was hungry, left them in their amusement and, still chuckling, went out to the shop across the street. He returned with several tins of corned beef, milk and a large loaf of bread. They laughed and feasted until sleep dragged them to bed.

Simone tapped the notes until her wrists hurt. The weeks began to pass more noticeably. Her self-doubt was being gradually pushed aside by the tension of expectancy. She returned early from school each evening. For long hours, she tapped and echoed the notes in Mr. James' fashion.

The image of the pan became grafted to her mind. Mentally, she tapped out Beethoven's Minuet; composed her own melodies, making them as difficult as she possibly could in order to stretch herself. Mr. James taught her portions of Busy Body. Thus she learnt how to make runs and how to extemporise on themes. He hounded her mercilessly for the mistakes she made. She couldn't tap the notes too hard or too softly. Nita also, herself becoming obsessed, began to butt in when she thought that something didn't sound 'right'. Simone could now close her eyes and tap any note she wanted.

The six weeks had passed. Mr. James was still not satisfied. He seemed confused, unhappy. Nita demanded that he get off his 'tail' and take them to meet 'dat Calinago Moose fella.' The two days before, she had begun preparing herself for what she thought was surely going to be a war with the bandleader. The woman was prepared to give Moose something more than a piece of her mind if he dared reject her daughter.

Mr. James took them along finally, with Nita leading the way to Tanteen. She shouted at them to hurry up. Mr. James complained that she was making him more nervous. He had himself to blame, Nita retorted.

Calinagoes was a wide, open tin shed with two bright gas-lamps hanging from the rafters. It stood at the edge of a large playing field. The space inside was packed with steelpans of all sizes. Most were hung on stands of steel piping. At the back were a set of drums whose cymbals and high hats glowed like full moons. On either side, near the corners stood two sets of full sized steel drums, six to each set, standing on wooden stands and ranged in a way that there was a narrow passage between each set. Pans of intermediate sizes were placed in neat lines in the center of the structure. At the front were the smallest pans, glittering chrome. The girl recognised them immediately. They were tenorpans. Mr. James' drawing had been perfect.

Several young men were grouped before the shed. They held sticks and seemed to be consulting in whispers, while they threw curious glances at Simone and her mother. Nita returned their gaze with unflinching malice. A group of four girls stood on the grass

several feet from the shed, chatting noisily among
themselves. Mr. James left them; returned with a
sour-faced young man. Tall and powerfully built, he
stood a head above Mr. James.

'That is the one?' he asked, pointing at Nita.

'So what happen if is me?' she shot back, aggressively.

'Naw, is not her — shh, Nita! Is this young lady, Af —
erm Simone.'

'And you say she could play?'

'She'z boss, man.' Mr. James didn't sound very sure
of himself.

'You could play?' The young man cast clinical eyes
over the girl.

'She could play, oui,' Nita affirmed.

'Y'know, I don' custom to no girls in my . . .'

'We went through that already,' Mr. James cut in
weakly.

'I givin' you a test,' Moose told her.

'You don' give them boys no test!' Mr. James pro-
tested.

Simone followed the man on shaky feet. He led her to
the back of the building where the big drums were.

The girls on the grass, sensing the drama, stopped
their chattering and drew closer.

Simone felt lost. The dryness in her mouth was
uncomfortable. She would have felt better if Mr. James
were with her.

'Run something on this.' Moose pointed at an old
tenorpan with signs of rust showing clearly on the rims.
Simone bent over the instrument. The light was weak in
that corner of the shed.

'Can't see the notes,' she said feebly.

'You need to see the notes?' Moose grumbled, sourly.

'Nuh . . . Not, not really.'

'Play then.'

She selected a note and touched it gently, humming
as she was used to. It responded immediately and she
recoiled, surprised. Until then, it was she who had
added the sound to the tapping stick. With great
deliberation, she touched each note, knitting her

brows unhappily when several notes refused to yield the expected sound.

'I thought you could play?' The band leader's voice was like a blast in her ears. Simone straightened up, clutching the sticks against her small chest.

Mr. James came to her rescue. 'You can't see that the pan is untuned, man? Is a condemned pan; so why you give 'er in the first case? Why she don't use one o' these tenorpans in front here?' He was pointing angrily at the shiny instruments in front.

Nita was saying nothing — a sure sign that she was working herself up to a state of uncontrollable wrath.

'C'mon, Af,' Mr. James whispered prayerfully.'Easy! Just relax and blast those buggers to pieces. O God, girl! You cant fail me now.' To Moose he said: 'Give her a chance, man. The youth not familiar wit' the arrangement of the notes. I always tell you fellas to standardise the goddamn instruments so that all the pans could be made the same. But nobody listen. Gwone, girl. Play fo' me.'

A young man suddenly detached himself from his companions and without being bid, drew one of the shiny instruments towards Simone. He smiled fleetingly at her and she felt better.

Again she began to explore the surface of the pan. The notes rang true. The girls who were now directly in front of her, seemed to be willing her to go on. Slowly at first, she began stringing the notes of a melody together. The tune grew louder, more coherent, as she grew in confidence. It trickled out of the instrument, became an easy stream, swelled and spattered in torrents of silver sound around her.

Simone did not hear the smattering of applause from the girls near her, or Nita's sudden shriek of delight. The girl looked up to see Mr. James tapping his feet rapidly, his body thrust forward with an eloquence she knew Nita and herself alone would understand. *Attack!* He was telling her. She felt strong and spiteful with Moose standing near her, hoping she would fail herself, her mother, Mr. James, and the girls standing close by who were her friends because they were saying so with their faces.

She began teasing from the pan, notes that were bright and round and clean like new coins. Smoothly, effortlessly, she launched into Busy Body holding the rhythm down with her feet and smiling.

The youth, who had earlier on placed the pan before her, made his way to the congas at the back of the shed. The rhythm came in on her gently as if anxious not to startle her. It then grew into a pulsating calypso tempo that never rose above the tune; stayed just beneath it, supporting, responsive, adding body to her music.

She stopped abruptly and left the music hanging and the group, unsated.

'We want her!' the drummer said, so that everyone could hear.

Moose didn't like the initiative being taken away from him. 'Not bad!' he said, looking at Simone who had not moved.

'Not bad? She damwelly good!' one of the girls replied.

'We take you for a couple months — on probation and if . . .'

'What! Proba-who?' Mr. James had suddenly become the man who had stood night after night pounding his music into Simone's head. 'Lissen, man. I can't tell you how to run your band. I not telling you now. But! If you ever try that I leave and never come back. I mean it.'

'I like de arrangement, man.'

'Dat is not de issue now!'

'She play it well. Right I take she.'

'No conditions?'

'No conditions.'

Good! You could count me in den.'

The young drummer — he called himself Steve — followed Simone around the shed naming the different pans for her.

'But you play in a band befo' and you don' know the difference between cello, double tenor, bass . . .'

'Yeh, I was too busy playin' to learn the name o' them

instruments.'

Moose was complaining to Mr. James, 'Now you give me real problems, man. All them little 'ooman going pressure me to take them in the band now.'

'Is time,' Mr. James answered, coldly. He threw his arms around the girl's and her mother's shoulders and jigged all the way home.

Nita's exuberance was shortlived. The man talked only of Carnival and winning the competition between the bands of the island with his Busy Body arrangement.

They went to practice everyday except on weekends. Nita tagged sullenly along, her mood worsening as, each night, they returned home late.

Simone had mastered the instrument and several calypsoes. She learnt quickly, applying Mr. James' initial teachings. More and more, she found herself explaining combinations to her companions. Try as she might though, she could not please Moose. He accused her everytime of adding her own 'colour' to the tunes. The other players claimed they liked her style, but Moose seemed to have many reservations.

Playing however, brought her a fullness never dreamed of before. She carried this special happiness even to school. And with the passing months, her satisfaction was completed by their preparations for Carnival. They polished pans, welded new stands together and added wheels to the floats that were to carry the instruments along the road during the festivities. She went more and more to the back of the shed in order to watch Steven play the six bass brums. The 'youth played every instrument in the band. On the bass, he would throw his arms back and forth, drawing heavy, healthly music with the two extra-large sticks tipped with balls of heavy sponge. It seemed incredible that a person could play six drums at the same time, but the boy did it with joy and confidence.

'You like that boy,' Nita told her, accusingly.

'Which boy!'

'De ugly likkle kobo-face' one.'

'I tell you I like 'im?'

'Don't give me no rudeness!'

'I like to *see* 'im play that's all.'

'You have yours to play, not so?'

'Tenor and bass different: them *look* different; them *sound* different!'

Mr. James' intervention was timely. She couldn't stop her now! That was what Simone was about to tell her. She couldn't stop her. There would be trouble if she tried. And that was all.

'Something not right with you,' Mr. James said that night, 'I feel it. I mean, you play like a queen. You play wit' conviction and everyt'ing and yet you not happy. Is not like dem fellas: when dem play is like the water o' life dat dey bend over to wash dem soul in. Dem play like if pan is the world. But you — you happy, yet you miserable. You find out what missin' from the minuet? No? Well, I *think* I know the problem. We goin' see!'

From then on she was allowed to play the bass drums on Wednesdays — the day Moose stayed home and left the band to James.

It was a new world — the big pans! They demanded everything of her, pulling and pushing her to and fro as she fought to stay with the tunes the band played. They drained her but she couldn't wait to return to them the following week.

Moose came unexpectedly one Wednesday and caught her. He just stood there staring incredulously with his hands on his hips. And to everyone's surprise, their leader passed the rest of the night teaching Simone to keep up with a calypso version of Beethoven's Minuet in G.

Busy Body had finally become the band's own. They had given it shape and colour. The runs were glorious, shooting in hot pulsing cascades into the night around them, drawing like moths, the small crowds that would later become regular, fanatical supporters of Calinagoes.

Simone grew on the bass as she could never have grown on the tenor-pan. Here was all the freedom she craved, all the movement that was both muscle and music. It was from playing the big drums that she drew admiring gasps from the increasing numbers of visitors. She was long, graceful; distinct against the shining drums; whip-like in the way she struck out at the notes; making music with an involvement that was infectuous.

The crowd of onlooking girls grew. They came to watch Simone; to rock, stagger and dance to her 'wicked bass-line.'

The band rehearsed up to the very morning of Carnival. Mr. James could neither eat nor sleep. A row had broken out between himself and Nita because she didn't want her daughter to play on the road surrounded by what was to her, a mass of jumping hooligans. That Simone would be with the band and protected by her companions, did not budge Nita one inch. Panorama — the steelband championship — was alright with her. But Simone was not to play on the streets.

Panorama came. Eight bands were lined up for the vast, floodlit island that was the stage. Calinagoes was fifth in line. Somewhere in that massive crowd waiting expectantly in the Queen's Park pavillion, sat Mr. James and Nita. Simone wondered if they were as tense as she was. There was no mistaking the rivalry between the bands. It was there in the smiles, in the sheen of sweating faces, in the tone of voices around her. Most bands had girl-players. Like her, they were neatly uniformed in the colours of their band. Simone eyed them; they eyed her. She smiled and they smiled back.

Finally her band rumbled on stage amidst complete silence. Calinagoes had been losers for the past three years and they were expected to lose again. The band stood glittering beneath the raw lights, statuesque, waiting for the word from Moose. The cue came and they attacked.

Calinagoes played. They played for Mr. James, for everything he'd taught them, for the hard times they'd given him, for the endless cursings he'd given them. They played for all the nights of pounding, shaping and polishing his arrangement. They played for the sake of music, for what it had done to them — for what it was still doing. And the images he had fed them of fire, steel and love were in the music. They played to win.

Calinagoes won.

It mattered little to Simone that the days following their victory were ones of intense celebration for her band. She spent the nights staring into the darkness, fretting over the minuet like a dog over a plastic bone.

J'Ouvert morning, while the strains of the minuet were pouring down on the town like a discordant shower, Mr. James took the two of them the short distance to Market Hill from where they could see herds of revelers pouring into St. George's from all directions.

The hum and buzz of the thousands below rose up, oblivious of the music from the hill above.

Jab-jabs, coated in oil and charcoal, stomped and intimidated the throngs of the onlookers. The air shimmered and throbbed with the colour and chant of Vecoup, Wild Indians, and Ole Mass, scandalising presidents, queens, priests, ministers: themselves; while Beethoven's Minuet taunted, asserted, defied, stopping only when the town withdrew for want to rest.

'The violence ain't finish yet,' Mr. James had said. 'Nor the love . . .'

She'd wondered what he'd meant by that. The love was making sense; she understood that part. But the violence? At first she thought it was the bloodshed — the killing laws that had sought to abort the birth of pan. Then she thought again of Moose's resistance to her joining his band and the struggle, over the months, to earn their acceptance. That too was violence, wasn't it? And now, that music from the hill which challenged everything — a rebuke in every note — why did it make her feel that way? She loved pianos, trumpets — everything! But this — this was not an act of love. It was a flag of rejection thrown out on the wind for all to notice.

Last year's mixed up images of pianos warring with pans, came back to her with added sharpness. She had to do something — to respond as forcefully as she could. And when she did, it would be for all those past years of submissive listening, and the recent months of searching, fighting, hungering for a language, to reply.

The next day, before leaving home, there was another terrible row with her mother. The roof shook with the defeaning power of Mr. James' voice. But before he could go on, Simone cut in sharply, brutally; knowing that this time, the fight was hers; that for some reason, it was *her* voice that mattered now and not Mr. James'.

'None o' you can't stop me!'

Mr. James stopped short, open-mouthed, surprised that Simone seemed to be including him.

'Y'all don't leave me alone, I walk out o' dis house and never come back.'

If it were anger, or even a challenge, Nita might have known how to deal with her daughter's resistance. But it was a coolness, a detachment she couldn't understand. She could not bear the rejection in her daughter's eyes.

'But Sim,' Nita pleaded, flapping her arms confusedly at her side and looking miserably at the man. Mr. James, though surprised, seemed equally detached.

'What kind o' modder you say you is — always tryin' to tie me down like that?'

Nita's deep hurt took some time to register.

'Okay, okay!' Mr. James muttered, placatingly.

'Gimme a chance. You always butting in when I talkin' wit' Nita. Is the last day o' carnival and nobody goin' prevent me from joinin' Nagoes on the streets. You always tryin' to stop me, Neets — why? Tell me.'

Her eyes fell on her mother's face and suddenly she became all filled with softness for her. Simone thought she understood her. But there were many things — many, many things she would no longer accept from Nita, or anyone else. No, Sir!

The girl turned abruptly and strode through the doorway. She heard Mr. James' brief grumbling to her mother, then his rapid footsteps behind her, trying to catch up.

*   *   *   *   *

The afternoon sun was hot on their necks when they prepared to roll. Masqueraders in glittering costumes were passing in busloads along the Tanteen road. It was a day of intense colour and movement. However, the afternoon was still subdued, hoarding its energy for the toss and tumble of late evening.

'Arrrigght!' hailed Moose, drawing the attention of the band and their hundred or so supporters scattered around the field. 'Remember, we is a people's band — anybody could join us'. He said this with special vehemence, since most of the other bands did not tolerate being invaded by uncostumed revelers before the daylight faded.

'Lissen to de strategy: we goin' into the City silent-silent. I don' want to hear a note from nobody till I say, GO! And when I say, GO! we hittin' dem hard. We de-vas-ta-tin them and is non-stop we playin'.' Moose turned to face the crowd, 'Those of you who pushin' the floats, remember: NO FIGHTIN' or quarrelin'. De only War Nagoes makin' today is with MUSIC! Everybody know the route we takin' so I not repeatin' it. Any questions?' Moose turned, confident that no questions would follow.

'Yes!'

'What happen now, Sim?'

'I wan' to make a request.'

'I not playin' no radio, you know,' said Moose.

'Lissen to the lady,' Mr. James cut in, good-naturedly.

'Say it, Sim.'

'When we reach Lucas Street I want us to play Minuet.'

'You crazy! Mornin' music?'

'Yep! We playin' it calypso style!'

'This is Carnival, man!'

'I say calypso-style,' insisted the girl.

Moose was in doubt. 'Well, if erm, if de fellas — fellas, you-all want to play morning music the last day o' Carnival?'

The band nodded, grinning; their grins becoming wider as Moose's bewilderment got the better of him.

Without a word he came across to Simone and handed her his bass sticks, pointing to his drums.

'Jam de bass. I beating tenor today. I 'fraid you!'

Simone scuttled over and planted herself between

the six drums lest Moose should change his mind.

They chose a quiet corner of the town to dry out after the long, hot haul across the Carenage.

Moose was a good general. He kept them on a tight leash, pumping the adrenalin into them with words that came in short, hot salvoes. He rallied them till they were snapping to break loose on the town. The church clock boomed, the order came, and the young men dug their heels into the asphalt, straining furiously against the wheeled floats. They began to move in a thunder of wheels and a sudden, dramatic eruption of the hottest calypso in the land.

They were on Young Street when the crowds began to pour in behind them. In minutes it became a massive, pulsing river, spilling over the sidewalks, swelling irresistibly as more people were swept off their feet into midstream.

The band played, feeding on the boundless energy generated by the sea of joyous, bouncing bodies behind and around them. They were no longer Calinagoes; they had become a single throbbing whole two thousand strong, afire in the streets of St. George's.

The hours passed; the lights went on. No one noticed. Simone was drunk with music. She played as the people moved: with a precise, controlled madness that was beautiful in itself, for itself. Her hands demanded and received sounds that were life and love and power all at the same time.

They were already eight hours on the road when the circuit, laid out for them by Moose, was almost completed. They spilled over into Lucas Street — Simone's street. Her moment had arrived.

The players remembered but did not slip immediately from the calypso, Soca Girl, to the minuet. In the relative quiet, above the faint heartbeat of the masquerading town, there came the strains of Beethoven's Minuet in G, challenging as usual, derisive.

Mr. James who had been content to dance close behind the band, his face glistening with sweat, looked up at her and grinned briefly.

'Arright fellas!' he shouted. 'The song — the song for Simone! One-two-three-four, GOOOO!!'

The drums went first. In rapid waves the tenor pans reacted. Then the rest of the band.

Simone picked up the rhythm with a vengeance. The crowd moved forward dancing and ad-libbing to the fierce calypso rhythm. She pounded the music out in hot flushes of anger. Catching her spirit, the players sent their notes riding high above the houses and the night. The church clock struck the half hour and that too became music. The girl was grimacing, her eyes closed. There were the tenors screaming majestically; the enraged congas, stammering; the scraper, teasing; the steel-rim clamouring and her bass drums belching thunder.

Simone played and laughed while the people danced and chanted, till midnight sounded the passing of Carnival. She was surprised to see her mother with her arms entwined around Mr. James' waist when they came to a halt in Market Square. Nita had changed her mind after all.

Moose came over, hugged and thanked her. He told her how wise he was to have invited her to join Nagoes; he always knew that girls would give his band a face-lift.

Once home, Mr. James chirped happily away till morning. The girl stretched herself out on the settee, sighing long, tense sighs. For the first time in her waking life the minuet did not come.

'They tired,' Mr. James yawned.

'Don' think so,' Simone said, softly.

'You special — you make for bass drums,' the man said, with something like wonder in his voice.

Simone smiled and drew her knees up to her chin.

Nita had left the house in a hurry when she did not hear the Old Birds' music coming from the hill. The girl was shivering slightly, awaiting her mother's return.

A couple hours later, Nita burst through the doorway. She was frightened. It was terrible, she said. She couldn't understand it. She had prepared everything for them to pass the holidays comfortably. And it had to happen like that — when she was not around to help. The old lady, she must have drunk something because when the police arrived, they found a bottle of some funny stuff next to her. And the old man was just there, sitting on the floor, crying and soiling himself, same as any child. He done gone right off his head now. Didn't even know where he was.

Simone had sat bolt upright, startled, even frightened by the news. Mr. James seemed less concerned. He was staring at the rafters expressionless, absorbed in his own thoughts. Simone wondered why he seemed so unaffected. Would he be able to explain — understand perhaps, her sudden twinge of guilt, replaced now, gradually, by a curious sense of ease? The morning was quiet, peaceful, except for the sound of Nita's high-pitched distress.

What was she going to do now? She didn' like dependin' on no man — and look at Simone self! Why the hell she grinnin' so funny? With those big, black eyes o' hers! If a person didn' know better they would think she had somethin' to do wit' . . . .

'I t'ink I know what missin' from dat music, Mr. James.'

'Yeh?'

'I talkin'! Nita screamed.

'Me too,' said Mr. James. 'You was sayin', Af?'

'No guts — dat's what. No drums, no real riddim, no bassline — dat's what.'

'No Africa?'

'Huh?'

'Never mind.'

The girl stretched, yawned, 'De drums . . . blow down the flippin' erm . . . de flippin' erm, leaf — touch ground now. De bass . . .' Simone sighed. Her eyes drooped and stayed closed.

'What dis little woman sayin?' Nita asked, puzzled.

'Everything,' said James. He paused a moment, puzzled by his own reply. 'Thaaz right,' he muttered with great finality, coming out of a long silence, 'Everything!'

Oleander Road

For Peti

'Home-home, home-home,' Damon breathed, cursing his feet because it was so hard to keep them going to the rhythm of his words.

An hour or so earlier, he had tried willing them on with the habitual, 'lep-right, lep-right!' but those commands seemed to slow him down even more. They reminded him all too powerfully of the things he'd left behind.

He no longer carried the uniform: the boots, the clothes and the A.K. 47 with which he and the nine others — mere children — had followed Lieutenant Toni into the war. For a while, he'd carried the Makarov prised from the horrifying coldness of the lieutenant's hand; but then, finding little relevance in holding on to it, he'd thrown the pistol away.

Toni had been the last to fall. He'd gone down shouting, 'Forward! Forward! For-' The last syllable had been blasted away by the grenade that came arcing through the bushes towards them. Such terrible cries, Jeezas! the children — children shouldn't go down like that. You closed your eyes and thought it was the earth screaming murder. And to think that somebody somewhere would be sitting there waiting, praying — crying perhaps — for their child's return.

If any of them were like his mother, he knew what they would be thinking now, pent up like prisoners behind their own bars of fear — hm, nice imagery; should put it in a poem some day. But for whom? There would be no more Councils — no more gathering of ears to listen to his poems. His own heroes had seen to that.

His mother had mouthed her anger at them. She'd thus uprooted them from inside herself and he'd felt that he too was a part of that rejection. Her logic was simple: you cannot expect to break your own people's heart, burn terror in their souls and when the enemy came, ask the very ones you've hurt to fight for you.

He wished it was that simple for him; wished he could have made her understand why he had chosen to go into the bushes and face, admittedly, the terror of an incoming army who'd claimed they came to save. Dragons, he'd told her, did not become saviours overnight. She'd watched him like a stranger then; her love, replaced by mockery. The gulf between them had become so great! But this, and this alone, explained his leaving home — nothing else. He believed in nothing now; only the road, cruel beneath his feet, and the need to reach home.

When the lieutenant had fallen, a stillness had come over everything. A strange expression remained frozen on his face — surprise? hurt? Or both? His open eyes were staring up, past the flares that rose in hot, orange flashes, searing the night sky; staring emptily, at nothing. In the distance, the guns were going off in murderous volleys of orchestrated hate. The acrid stench of burnt sulphur stung his nostrils; and for the first time, he knew the scent of human blood.

He was alone in the bush — in all the world — hurting where the piece of shrapnel had pierced him. Yet there he was, not thinking how lucky he was to have tripped and fallen just seconds before the bomb landed. No! He'd just stood over his friends — so stupified, he couldn't even cry — half-hoping they would get up and laugh as children do, assuring him that it was just a game and it was time for home. He'd stood there a long time, staring.

He was not hurting now — just a numbness at the side. He'd stripped himself naked, except for the underpants and the once-green T-shirt, tied clumsily around his waist.

He concentrated on his stride, no longer wondering if the war would end, no longer grieving at the loss, or searching himself for answers to questions that had begun haunting him days before the bombs, the planes and gunships landed.

'Home-home!' He had to keep walking — couldn't stop; else, he would never find the will to start off again. Sleep would grab him. Not having slept for three days, it was coursing through his veins like liquor. He'd read a story once — couldn't remember by whom — Steinbeck? It was about a man — an old fella — who believed that as long as he kept on his feet, kept on the move, he would forever escape the downward clutch of age.

Damon did pause however to look confusedly around, trying to figure out the distance he had covered; hoping thus, to find assurance in the fact that he had made some progress.

Dishearteningly, he had only covered the little hill that led, a mile back, to the bushes, the grasslands; and just beyond, the battlefield. He wished he could know the time, to the exact second. In some curious way, he felt it was important — something he had to know in order to cover the next mile. It should be close to morning he thought, because the sliver of the moon that hung like a piece of fingernail over the nearest hill, was almost down.

Behind that hill, he'd left his friends, and a memory he would write about someday.

He'd emerged from the bushes and come upon a squad of youths crouching in the dark. It wasn't cold but some were shivering. Didn't know what to do; had no orders, they said. They were unable to establish radio-contact with anyone. They didn't even know how things were going. And why should they be there anyway when most of the people had remained at home; had not even bothered to come out and fight?

One of the girls had bandaged him with deft but trembling hands. She'd marvelled at his luck. They could have shot him by mistake on hearing him come through the bushes. She wasn't complaining, she'd muttered, but she couldn't help thinking of her Pepi. He would be awake now, clamouring to be fed. She was hoping that those at home could cope with the child while she was away. Where was he going? she'd asked finally, looking doubtfully at his wound.

'Oleander Road,' he'd answered, 'a few miles from here — not far. You know where I mean?'

She nodded vaguely, unconvinced. She'd given him her hand just before following her group with furtive care through the bush, heading for the screech and thunder in the distance. He would always remember her. Nina — Nina Louis was her name.

'Mus' be delirious or somethin',' Damon thought, because he couldn't recall when he'd started walking again. The road stretched long and grey before him in the early-morning dusk. Now, it felt soft — cushionlike. His anxiety was replaced by a sense of airiness, of exiliration even, as he felt himself springing forward; not minding if the familiar landmarks at the roadside were seeming to crawl by with infinite slowness.

This road, he mused, never thought of it like this before: first, cruel, then kind, now treacherous.

He lived at the other end. As a child, he used to play marbles and spin tops on it. Now it was the road, that spun; not the tops. He was forced to step more carefully. He used to like sleeping on its warm surface just before the sun went down. It would ooze warmth like a body and the vehicles that rarely passed, would stop a few yards off and wake him with their horn.

He passed the little church on his right. He was christened there. The cemetry was just behind it. Soon there would appear the houses of Miss Maggie, Tizie, then Jo-Jo. The last name tiggered off an old memory.

Once, Mr. Jo-Jo almost chopped his hand off; just for a rotten piece of cane he'd tried to steal from the man's garden. Whack! — the cutlass had come whistling down, barely missing his wrist. Not his left hand — no! But the one he wrote with. Had he chopped it off, there would have been no poems, no 'forward-ever' slogans on the walls, houses and culverts of Oleander Road; neither joy nor miracles expressed with pen or paint. Not that it mattered now. The time of miracles, of making flowers grow on stones, and the sun rise in children's eyes, had been crushed beneath a storm of guns.

He was hurting again. The pain was in his legs and chest. The road became unsteady, teetering like a boat below him. It had always been a steady road, dependable, tame. Now it was rebelling against him, resentful of his very presence, it seemed.

Country road, take me home to the place where I belong . . . The rest of the song refused to come to him. He'd heard it somewhere — couldn't remember where. The radio, perhaps.

Damon came to a place where the road twisted sharply, directly below an overhang of rocks. A small wall on either side marked where the culvert ran under the road. He couldn't see the walls clearly, but he knew the words he'd painted on them were still there — in burning red — beneath a painting of farmers, workers and children reaching for the open skies with clenched fists: *BREAKING CHAINS TO CHANGE!* He used to be proud of those words. He had thought them up himself.

Damon made out the shapes of houses. His mind told him they were near; his feet, fighting him now, were protesting at the distance. The smell of oleanders, painfully sweet, filled his head. They grew at the side of the road, their stems stained dark, and gnarled, with age. Strange but beautiful! these flowers which bloomed in fragrances of purple, white and pink at any time they chose.

This year, they chose October. For most of the year, the roadside would be somber-green, then suddenly, it would become all sweet and dressed up and bridal. Jeez! And to think they'd almost cut them down.

It was during the Festival of Work. The whole country was on its roads, chopping, digging, cleaning, paving — a glorious time! He had done a good job, mobilising the village. That weekend, everyone came out, and the village worked and joked and sang!

It was strange what this hunger for sleep was doing to him. He was not just remembering; he felt as though he was actually slipping back into time.

On the first day, they were assessing the work to be done on Oleander Road. A young engineer had come from the Ministry to advise.

'We have to widen this road,' he said. 'Cut down those rhododendrons and pave it with pitch. These cobblestones won't do; they can't take the weight of heavy vehicles. You see, comrades, Oleander Road is going to be what we call a major artery that will link the two main roads — Westerhall and the Eastern Main, right?' He went on to speak of developing infrastructure, increased gross national product and productivity.

Damon laughed. It came out as a short gasp, as the pain suddenly tightened it grip inside him.

Mr. Jo-Jo was good for something after all, 'You mad, man!' he said to the engineer. 'Widen the road? And cut down dem Rosebay tree?' He was pointing at the extremely tall growths of oleander. 'Naaaw! Excuse me disrespeck, sonny; but you dunno what you sayin!'

It was mainly the old men and women who were prepared to put up a fight. But Tizie brought the rest round with her explanation. The road, she insisted, should not be changed. Why not? Because it was meant to stay that way. 'You see, once it had a war when all o' we people wuz slave. Is what my decease modder tell me. We did want to break away from slave-master' rule, cause wuz worst than hell. But dey won't let we go, unless we did fight dem. Some of us had to dead for some to live, you-all unnerstan?'

'Well, it had this man who make big, big war. We start makin' hell in dis place — fire, blood an' brimstone! It last months — months! Because dem who did want to go on ownin' us, bring big army from overseas-country to help dem fight back. Dem come wit' gun an' cannon. We never had no gun, only cutlass and fire, so we start losin' de war; had to retreat. In those times, dis place wuz big forest. We had to run and hide quite-quite up in those bush-mountains behind up there. Dis road uses to lead right up to them mountain. We had to make it first; cut right through the forest one night, to get away from cannon an' gun-powder-shot. Y'all won't believe it, but we gran'parents make dat road in one night! Those who survive — a long time after, dey decide to plant these rosebay tree here to remember, coz rosebay, never does dry up an' die; it keep growin' or else it send up anodder shoot to take it place. All you young people never does ask no question; y'all just want to chop-down. Well, you goin' have to chop us down first coz we is de children-children o' dem same people who plant dem flowers right there.'

In those times, Damon thought, the wounded wouldn't have felt so alone; they would have been together, carried by hands that underscored that unity with love. He — he was alone.

He was just passing Tizies' house and was still reflecting on her story. She had been so happy, after-wards, that her words could still change some things: more precisely, that she could stop some things from changing.

Something else was revealed — a warning from Jo-Jo. Lovely as they were, oleander trees were poison.

'If you cut them down and de sap go in your eye o' mouth, you'z a dead man! It spoil you' blood for good! Is like we: we nice until you try to cut us down; then we turn poison.' They'd laughed then, so softly, with such confidence, you felt they'd made the world and were themselves just as permanent.

Not long after, a poem had come to him, an imperfect one he'd thought; but he'd never sought to polish it. It was just a thought, a feeling; now, a kind of crucifix, strung together by words. How did it go? How — 'We' yes! 'course!'

We never knew — these feet that fell so fast — for home — were walking on a past — of flowers, stones — and bones! Our mountains did! — and now have sent us down to seize our day — and in our turn — be claimed by sun — the flowers and the stones — of Oleander Road!

It did mean something after all. It did!

His house was not far away. Perhaps if he called, they would hear him. He called, but could not hear his own voice, he felt so weak.

The road was soft again. If he lay down for a while, surely his strength would return. Damon couldn't help wondering if the old man was still wandering around the world, and if so, where was he now? And that girl — that girl he'd met in the bushes, was she as angry as he? As hurting with betrayal? Did she still believe? Or would she, like he, discard her gun, her uniform and return to her Pepi who might still be crying. About all that, a poem would someday come. No one might want to hear it; but that was alright. The poem will still be his.

Abandoning the struggle with his feet he let the road claim him. It warmed his whole body, gently. Its warmth was almost humanlike. Damon closed his eyes, smiling, the beginnings of a poem stirring in his head — a beautiful one, rich with the sap of oleander bush.

'It goin' take some time,' he sighed, 'before it finish. My modder will have to wait fo' me a li'l longer.' He smiled again and no longer heard the muffled thunder of cannons in the south.

The Room Inside

The doctor didn't come. He'd refused to. Well,he just said he was tired; and, didn't they know that doctors needed sleep too?

Yes-yes! 'course they'd told him that the nurse wasn't there, the Medical Station was locked — as the care-taker had explained — because a man had almost half-killed his wife in Roebuck and Nurse Finchley had gone there to look after the woman.

They thought he might have changed his mind and come after all. But his wife had heard them and come to the doorway. She reminded him that he had just finished having the car fixed and it had just enough petrol to take her to the wedding the following day.

Wedding, yes! That was what she said. One of her friends. Said she had to do the flowers o' somethin'. She complained 'bout the weather too. Impossible, she said. All this rain and thunder made the road bad for cars. Besides, a doctor could break his leg climbing this slippery hill. Hope Vale was a bad place anyway — yes, that's what she said, — a bad place; even in the best weather. Didn't everyone know about the landslides that came sweeping suddenly down to block the old road, trap vehicles and crush, like biscuits, the houses in their paths.

She said she blamed him. It was his fault. Hadn't she often warned him about spoiling those people with his kindness? It didn't pay to be so nice to them, thus opening himself to their abuse.

They *did* tell Dr. Raeburn that it was a delicate matter; that Elaine was a sickly girl and the child was coming early. They simply couldn't get her to the

hospital in time. He'd become really angry then; shouted that they could not blackmail him, his hands were
clean and no two so-and-soes could open his gate, walk
into his yard and stand there, soaking wet, in his
verandah, trying to make him do what he didn't have to.
He was a doctor; not a midwife.

They were in the yard — a tight circle of men, women
and children. The rain was beating down in hard, white
sheets as if intent on pounding them into the soft mud.

The two youths who had run the five miles to St.
Paul's and back, fidgeted nervously, digging their naked
toes into the wet earth, with the helplessness of children.

The three women drilled them with questions until
they had learned every detail of the boys' trek through
the storm, to the Medical Station, the doctors house his
rejection and their even hastier return.

Three of the youths had left together but only Ray
and Mike had returned. Jim, more determined than the
rest, had taken the road for St. Georges, to the hospital.
He'd done so only after calling at the two houses with
telephones, a couple of miles up the road. The lines, it
seemed, had been broken by the storm, and for some
reason, cars were hard to come by; their owners even
harder to persuade to venture down the forbidding
road.

St. Georges was ten miles away. Jim would be a long
time in arriving — far less returning in time — despite
his long stride and much admired stamina.

Nana lifted her eyes; seemed to search the water-
logged sky for something. The rain, pelting viciously
down, hit her hard in the face. She winced but did not
shift her gaze till she appeared to find what she was
seeking. Patsy, Elaine's mother, had that same expression of torment. But was quiet. The only evidence of her
fear for her daughter was in the slow heaving of her
massive chest. And her eyes — they were as dull as the
pools of water settled in the mud at her feet.

The third woman was Aya, Nana's older sister. She

stood slightly above them all, tight-lipped, tense; making and unmaking bead-loops with the chaplet around her neck.

Gigi observed them, sensing that something was wrong. Nobody had to tell her that. Nana's face was always like that when something dreadful was anticipated. Only this time it seemed worse because everyone was seized by the same unease.

Cecil was weeping. He was Elaine's boyfriend; and she, in child for him. It was impossible for Gigi to distinguish the tears from the rain, washing down his face.

But why was everyone so still, standing in the wind, the rain and thunder as though afraid to move? Why were they talking about Elaine here in Nana's — her mother's — yard when the girl was, according to them close to dying in the little house a hundred yards or so further up the hill.

Nana did not shoo the children away; she didn't even see them — her mind was so far away. In a sudden fit of self-consciousness, Gigi observed that she too was standing exactly as the adults were: arms akimbo, feet rooted in mud; suspended in a strange, uncertain tension that was worse than any discomfort she had ever known.

'Okay,' Nana breathed. They had all been waiting for her word. 'No choice! Is for we to do something. We have to bring Elaine down here'. She spoke with a blunt finality that brought relief to those around her. 'De only person I know who could do something now is my modder — the Old Lady. But first, I want Patsy to agree, 'cause I don' know what might happen. We could leave Elaine there to dead or we could *do* something. Tell me if you agree for my modder to deliver the child?'

Mutely, Patsy nodded her acceptance. Nana spoke with greater strength now and a sureness that reminded Gigi of the times her mother bathed her with hands whose scouring roughness was in itself, an expression of her gentleness.

'Aya, I want you to talk to the Old Woman. Tell er — tell er what the problem is: dat Elaine child comin' early;

dat you know is years now she stop deliverin' — since
that blasted nurse report her sayin' dat she not in no
medical 'Sociation and ain't qualify. Careful how you
say dat 'cause it still hurt her when she 'member how
they stop 'er from doin' she calling. You lissening? Okay!
But! we don't have nobody else round here to do it. And
most important, tell her that Patsy — the girl modder —
agree to have her deliver the child. She might refuse so
you will have to threaten and argue. Once she unnerstan, she goin' do it. If she still refuse tell her that *I* say
she *must* do. Dis is stickin-togedder-time. All o' we is
one on dis man' hill. Gwone!'

Aya looked fervently at Nana's face and, still fondling
her chaplet, marched into the house.

'De men — where the men? I don' want no boys for
dis; is men I want. Now you fellas, go to every house on
dis hill and tell the men, I want them. If anybody drunk
or been sleepin, leave dem' cause I don' want no more
problems. I want at least four strong men. Tell dem to
meet me on top of the hill by Patsy house and to bring
'long wit' dem the biggest and cleanest sheet they could
find in deir house. Y'all still standin-up there? Gwone!'

The boys scattered hurriedly, running in every direc-
tion and bellowing commands at each other, through the
rain, to better co-ordinate their mission. Nana glared at
the children, noticing them for the first time.

'Go home!' she snapped. 'Y'all want to ketch cold?
Y'all modder know where y'all is? Break that stick for
me, Gigi — GIGI!! What you doin' there, child? What the
. . . .! Nana lunged at them, swearing. The children
bolted off through the slippery mud, for home. Gigi had
nowhere to go to. Without being told, she realised that
once Elaine was brought down, her mother's house
would be completely out of bounds.

She sought shelter beneath the ant-blighted grapefruit tree which leaned directly over, and partly sup-
ported the little house. Her teeth chattered with the
coldness of her dripping dress.

Cecil was still distraught. He seemed lifeless, drained. The young man placed himself beside the little girl
beneath the tree. Water was streaming down the thick-
leaved branches. He took the dripping onslaught pas-

sively while Gigi strived to dodge the heavy drops. It would have been a game, the effort worth enjoying, had there not been this strange tension hanging over them more perversely than the ugly day. There were a few things she felt she had to know.

'Ces?'

'Huh?' The young man did not look at her. He was rubbing his small growth of beard as though it were bothering him.

'Erm — Elaine sick bad?'

He did not answer her. She persevered, 'She deadin — she goin dead?'

'What de hell you askin' me, gyul!' His anger was cool.

'Nana say she makin' a baby.'

'Dat don' mean she goin' dead,' he reproached; but there was no mistaking the fear in his voice.

'Y'all could tell Papa God to take back de baby; not so? Well, he don' bound to send it *now* if it make her sick. Y'all could ask im to keep it fo' you till she get better; not so?'

She couldn't understand why he was smiling so secretly, to himself. There she was trying to help and the stupid fella was pretending to ignore her advice! It made sense, didn't it? If having the baby sent meant so much problems for them all, then they should tell Papa God they wouldn't take it anymore. He would understand; wouldn't he?

'How come Elaine sick and you not sick? Is only cry you cryin' but *you* ask to be de fadder; not so? — you should be deadin too . . .'

'Shut up if you don' know what you sayin.' What likkle gyul like you want to know 'bout dat anyway? Move! before I clout you.'

'Joke! I tell my modder — she break you' head wit' one cuff!'

Cecil turned his back to her, brushing — with rapid, furious strokes — the water from his hair.

'Next mont',' said Gigi, 'I goin' ask Papa God for *four* baby. But I don' want Im to make me fat like Elaine. I want only girls — dolly-girls. What Elaine ask for — a boy? Tell me nah!'

Cecil never managed to tell her. Aya was at the doorway calling; 'Gigelle, come in from de rain — look at the child clothes, Lord! Cecil, why you don't shelter below de house? Elaine will be arright. Don't worry, son.'

Aya's voice was always gentle, so soft — as if forever on the verge of song. She could sing beautifully — songs of sadness and joy, of clouds and sunlight.

'Come here, Gi!'

Gigi ran into the house.

The woman set about stripping her and wiping her small body with gentle but thorough strokes of an old towel. Her grandmother's mumbling could be heard in the little room next door. Hers was a never-ending conversation with herself, broken only when she was eating or speaking to someone else.

Aya dressed the by now, deeply puzzled child in her best dress, stepped back and, after eyeing her critically, uttered softly, 'Dunno if you modder goin' like dis, Gi. Nana have she ways and I have mines. But we goin' need you. I don' think de lesson too big fo' you either! Light the coalpot — you gran'modder say she goin' need hot water, plenty of it. Make sure you hand cleaner dan a whistle when you boil that water.'

Moments later, the fire was going and the largest pot in the house placed on it. The other pots were filled and waiting. She worked with the sense of fighting to stave off some pending threat, made more awesome by the fact that she knew little or nothing of its true nature; only what she'd gathered from the curious gestures, the expressions of concealed turbulence printed on the faces of those around her.

There came a babble of voices above the sound of wind-swept rain, machine-gunning on the roof. She beat Aya to the door.

They were bringing Elaine down in a sheet. Each of the four men held a knotted corner of the large white piece of linen. Uncle Arthur, the giant, and Mr. Joe were at the front. Mano, the mute, was straining beside Nathan at the back. The sheet swayed ponderously and was balooned inwards with the weight of the girl.

During dry weather, the narrow dirt-track led all the way to the top of the hill. Now, there were only slipping mud and dark, running water. Sometimes the men were forced to sit on the wet ground, holding the make-shift hammock high, allowing themselves — under Nana's hawk-like surveillance — to slide down till they reached a lower, more secure level. The younger men and women stood clear of the men, darting in to help whenever they were called to, then backing clear off the path of the struggling four.

Every now and then, a sharp gull-cry came from the depths of the swaying sheet and Nana's voice became more insistent, urging the men forward. Gigi felt pride and fear and sadness whenever Nana's voice came to her through the rain. She felt so much like crying and she couldn't say why.

Finally, they were in the yard. Cecil hung over the sheet like a condemned man. Nana smiled at him with a solemn reassurance which served rather, to heighten his expression of helplessness. The girl was brought inside. The men returned, breathing sighs of tentative satisfaction.

Nana stopped Cecil at the door, turned and faced the group in the yard. There was something cold, almost insulting in the way she addressed them.

'Dunno what we'd ha done widdout you-all. But I dont want nobody hangin' around here while this bizness goin' on. GO HOME!! I not sayin' so twice. Just leave and go . . .'

'And pray fo' us,' Aya added, 'if de spirit move y'all.'

'Right!' Nana's interjection didn't seem to please Aya very much. 'You — Cecil, I know how you feelin' but you goin' have to find you'self somewhere else. I dont want no man 'round here; this is woman bizness! GIGI . . .'

She boiling the water. We goin' need her. She goin' stay in de hall.' Aya's tone was unusually firm.

Nana frowned at the sky. Her muse was cut short by the Old Lady's high-pitched voice demanding their presence. Gigi retreated with her mother, Aya and Miss Patsy into the house. Her mother locked the door.

The night was a long one, punctuated by Elaine's pain-ridden protests, the soothing music of Aya's voice, the wind, the rain and the old woman's muttering.

Gigi kept the fire burning low. The smoke stung her eyes and helped to keep the sleep at bay. She must have dozed off because at one point her mother was shaking her.

'Water!' she said. Quickly, the girl stirred and filled the outstretched basin. Nana rushed into the room. It must have continued like this for an eternity: filling and refilling the basin, placing the other pots on the fire to boil, waiting dutifully for Nana's insatiable demands for water.

Elaine must have wanted her baby really bad, the child thought. To be groaning and crying so much for it. Papa God was long in handing it to her. Mebbe he was still searching the sky for the right one to give her. The girl was too impatient though! She should learn to wait and not to suffer herself like that. Besides, it wasn't fair; Cecil should share some of the suffering too. Anyway, Elaine should learn to wait, and not to be so greedy. Gigi reconsidered her decision to ask for four babies the following month. Mebbe it wasn't so wise after all. Four might be too much. She should wait until she was as big as Nana.

The storm was over; the house, cool with the deep breaths of wind that made the branches of the grapefruit tree scrape harshly against the roof. The women had been talking in subdued tones when there came a sudden flurry of activity followed by her mother's firm command:

'Now.'

'Hold on love,' crooned Aya. 'Make an effort. Come on.'

Nana's approach was more businesslike. 'What you relaxin' for? I cyah do it for you. Come on, child!'

Miss Patsy's voice came: 'I holdin' you, Elaine.'

The old woman ordered them to shut up.

The little girl shut her eyes tight, absorbing the drama in the room. She heard Nana laugh and the strangeness of the sound shook her. Elaine was now silent. Patsy came for more water. The old lady muttered. They laughed.

The silence strained her. There came no baby-cry, no sign, nothing to justify the fragments of relieved laughter.

'At least the girl goin' be awright,' said Nana.

'But the child . . .' Aya sounded unable to say the rest. The rest of the sentence trailed off like smoke into the night.

Whispers came from the room. Gigi was seized by an odd sense of disatisfaction, of joylessness; because there was nothing rewarding in the tones of the voices coming from the room. Aya's face was strange when she came out.

'Come, Gi. You want to see?'

The child got up nervously, wondering about her mother's reaction to her presence in the bedroom. Aya took her by the shoulder and led her in.

Elaine lay prostrate on the bed, covered and asleep, it seemed. Beside her was a small doll-like thing all pink and curled up and perfect. Nana had seen her come in but did not appear to mind. The old woman was complaining to herself about doctors who didn't allow her to practice her calling and didn't come when they were really needed. And there she was now, with this, the failure of her life having to haunt her for the rest of her days.

Gigi couldn't figure out their problem. Nor was she able to find clarification in what was being said. She edged toward the bedside and with profound wonder, touched Elaine's baby — the toes, the hands. She found herself liking their softness. They were smooth — more smooth than warm.

'Is not my fault if de child didn't live.'

Gigi recoiled as though struck in the face. She understood everything from then on. Nana lifted it, wrapped it, brought it outside the hall and placed it on the 'atamah' near the fire. She stood over the small motionless bundle for a long, silent time, sighed heavily and went back in.

The little girl stooped and fondled the bundle timidly, hoping that by touch, she could better understand what the old lady had just said. Nana always told her that a person must never beg. It was not good — better to do without. Elaine must have begged too hard. The women were already discussing what they should do. They would need the men to dig a place for it. Funny! if they had to send it back, it should be sent up — back to where it came from; not further down. There was no sense in that. But . . .

'NAAA?!'

'Yesss!' Her mother's voice came low, irritable.

'Nana, it movin.'

'What! Doin' what?'

The four women seemed to shoot out from the room at the same time. 'What you sayin?'

'Watch, it belly movin.'

Miss Patsy took the bundle in her massive arms while Aya massaged it with great gentleness.

They hustled back into the room, consulting intensely with the Old Lady. A sharp slap from Nana and it wailed a long, piercing baby-wail.

It must have been morning when they ushered Gigi out, into the hall. The early birds were warbling in the grapefruit tree. The wind had subsided. Laughter gurgled like warm water from the room. Someone knocked the door. Gigi opened it to see Cecil standing there, dry now, but still very frightened.

'She awright?'

'Who Elaine?'

The young man nodded.

'Yep, think so.'

'An' — An' . . .' He couldn't say it.

'What?'

'Lemme come in.'

'You sleep?'

'Lil bit.'

'I didn' sleep!'

'Lemme come in. I wan' see my girl. She awright?'
'You don want to know about de baby?'
'Yes — move lemme come, nah! Step aside before I..'
'Before what? Nuh, you can't come in.'
'Is my girl.'
'Is a lil' girl.'
'I want to see me ooman. MOVE!!'
'Nuh!'
'Why not?'
Gigi remembered her mother's words to the men in the yard last evening.

'Dunno — is woman bizness.' She shut the door in his face, gently; retreated quietly and crouched before the fire, listening happily to the voices in the room and Aya's song, softly sung, of sweetness, life and sunlight.

The Canebreakers

. . . . no-no-no! No regrets. You see, it was something more than just an idea, really. Was, erm a kind of responsibility if you like: a legacy. Something my sister pointed me towards and kept on pointing at, over the years, till I suddenly stopped staring at her finger and really looked to see where she was pointing.

In fact, I've been thinking that it will be your turn soon. We need doctors now; builders, menders — makers of new roads. And always, I think, people like my sister to keep pointing out the way. Y'all unnerstan — No? Never mind. It will make sense as I go along. Just sit up and listen.

I used to watch the women coming home from work, wading ever so heavily, ever so tiredly, through the thick, orange light, their frocks fluttering like wide, grey wings. I would stand on the only, giant boulder in our yard and from there, peer down and over the fields of sugar cane searching among that crawling line for my sister.

I strived to pick her out, not by her face — dusk and distance wouldn't allow it — but by that long stride of hers and the curious way her body angled forward when she walked; as though pushing against winds felt only by herself. But they were no more than evening shapes, dark against the white feeder road that stretched way behind and beyond them till the distance narrowed it to a needlepoint.

'Sis', I asked once, when she reached home, 'why I could never mek you out from 'mongst all dem odder wimmen, comin home from work?'

I remember asking with great solemnity, affected as usual, by the air of seriousness that she perpetually carried with her, almost like another garment.

'Coz wee'z de same, Ah s'pose', she answered, pausing to consider, then repeating: 'Yep, wee'z de same. 'Sides, y'all men never choose de right light to look for us in.'

I didn't know what she meant by that. In fact, I didn't know what she meant by most of the answers she gave to my questions. The truth is, my sister hardly ever talked straight. Most people thought she never talked at all. For me, whenever she did, it was to say things that confused me greatly.

I used to think it was the canes that had her like that. I mean, any person would feel small and confused and lost in those puny, spider-legged houses of ours, standing like so many ugly, four-sided crafts at the very edges of a wild, green, tossing ocean of sugar canes.

Dry season, the time of reaping, she became more firm-lipped and even more silent than before. It was not like a sudden change of mood. Rather, it was something that happened slowly, a sort of deepening inside that grew with the growing of the canes, with their foam-like blossoming and, finally, their ripening in dry season.

I sometimes looked at Sis and found myself wondering about my mother. I couldn't recall what she looked like; though people said my sister was her spitting image. I must have missed her because I sometimes dreamt of this woman, of indistinguishable features, who had returned from Trinidad and taken me back there with her to meet a step-father, a brother and a little sister I had only heard about.

It was rumoured that Sis had been given the chance to live with my mother and she had not taken it. It was the year after Ma had left us. I was four; my sister, eighteen.

The boat ticket had arrived from Trinidad and my sister's departure date was confirmed. Farewell kisses and speeches were thrown at her like confetti. She had taken it all in, impassively, and had left the following morning dressed for Trinidad, clutching the brown cardboard suitcase in her right hand.

Imagine the confusion then, when about half an hour or so later, the workers on the estate saw her come in the taxi she had left with, borrow a machete and set to work, still dressed in her best dress; as if leaving for Trinidad and returning twenty minutes later were the most natural things in the world. She had said one of those puzzling things that I had, by now, grown accustomed to hearing from her.

'You have *ter break* cane, not *escape* cane. Somebody have to stay. Sides, it have cane in Trinidad too.'

She had taken me back — from my aunt's — to live with her in the house my mother had fled.

Sis got up very early every morning, waking me also. It would be so still, you could hear the canes rubbing leaves and get the smell of burnt sugar and rum from the big sugar factory miles away. She told me where to tie the goats for the day. And while I was out, she prepared the day's lunch — mainly boiled vegetables, salt'fish and a hot drink of black sage leaves or lemon grass which also served as breakfast.

She then tied her head and wrapped a strong band of cloth around her waist. Barefoot and straight-backed, she would stride out into the morning, the little machete held easily in one hand, the old, fire-blackened tin marked DANO MILK which contained her lunch, cupped carefully in the other.

She never said goodbye. But I didn't mind, because she was that way and I had grown accustomed to her silence.

Later, I would leave for school, balancing my books with the same care that Sis had held her cutlass; my lunch, in an identical can, carried in the other hand.

I never discussed school with Sis. She never asked. I simply told her what I wanted and she got it. I would hand her the slip of paper, folded exactly as the teacher had given it, with the name of the book he had scribbled there. Sis would take it delicately between her fingers,

as though afraid of hurting it and, without glancing,
place the note where she kept the little things she valued
— her money mostly — in the cleft of her bosom.

One night, I woke up and caught her staring at the slip
I had brought from school with 'The Students Com-
panion' written in my teacher's bold handwriting. She
did not know I was awake and studying her face in the
lamplight. I will never forget that picture of her, sitting
on the edge of the little bed, squinting at the paper, her
lips forming, ever so slowly, ever so painfully, letters,
words — a wish? It must have been half an hour before
she sighed, folded the slip carefully and placed it on the
bedside table.

That very Saturday, she got up early, put on what I
had come to call her 'Trinidad dress' and left for St.
George's on foot.

She returned in the afternoon with the new book and,
like all the times before, asked me to open it while she
sat in the corner, near the window, staring at me with
such a strange expression, I felt nervous and proud and
foolish at the same time.

I used to take these things for granted — I mean,
getting up on mornings, tethering the goats, watching
the people leave their homes and head like a great, long
column of worker ants, for the vast stretches of estate
cane that fed the sugar factory in the south.

You see, cane was always there and we expected to
live and burn our lives out in the fields — less abruptly,
perhaps, than my father who had passed away after
being hit by a lorry carrying cane. My mother? Well, she
gave up . . . .

I was always home before Sis. Having brought the goats
in, I did my homework sitting on the doorstep, hastening
to finish it before the rest of the daylight faded. Then I
climbed the boulder and watched for her.

Arriving, she would lower herself on the steps and I
would hand her the big, white enamel cup brimming

with water. My sister drank with a thirst — a grate-
fulness — I envied because she seemed to get such
pleasure from a cup of water!

If working for the estate made water taste so good;
that, for me, was reason enough to want to spend my life
there also.

'You sister don' wan' you to work on no estate,' Tin Tin
told me once.

Tin Tin was my friend — somebody I talked to and
day-dreamed with, freely. We were the same age and
shared so much of our spare time together, I often forgot
she was a girl who was therefore not supposed to throw
stones, climb trees, pick fights and steal sugar canes.
Yet, she could do all of these better than I. Worse, I
couldn't beat her in a fight and was oftentimes obliged
to retreat quickly into silence whenever our quarrels
became too heated.

'My sis didn' say she don' wan' me to work on no
estate,' I replied.

'She don' have ter, chupidy! She sen' you to school.
Give you eddication; not so?'

'Your modder sen' you to school too!'

'Yes, but she don' expect me to — well, she not
workin' she soul-case out fo' me. My modder diff'rent,
see! Is you an you' sister alone; my modder hav' eight o'
we. Sides, my fadder pass away.'

'My fadder pass away too!'

'Yes, but not in no sugar factory. Is a li'l ole truck dat
bounce yours. Mines, is a whole factory!'

'Factory don' bounce people,' I retorted, annoyed.

'I didn' say dat,' Tin Tin was getting annoyed too.

'Nuh, but you implied that. If you assert . . .'

'Ass — sert,' she echoed scornfully. 'Big wud; you
start showin' off!'

'De wud jus slip,' I apologised.

'Slip what! You jus' showin' off coz you sister buy you
big book an' you done scholarship exams. You know
damwelly if . . . .'

She stopped short. But I knew what she was going to say. She was brighter than I. She used to be in the same class as I until the Accident. Would have been doing the exams too, had not her mother said that it made no sense. The two biggest boys would have to work in the fields alongside her and she — Tin Tin — was not going back to school 'coz she couldn' afford no school-expense and there wuz two little children to take care of durin' de day.

'Sis, how come Tin Tin cyah go back to school?'
'Ask 'er.'
'She tell me arreddy'
'Don' ask me, den.'
'She bright.'
'I know dat.'
'Nearly bright as me.'
Sis looked at me. This was one of the times when I felt she didn't like me at all.
'Nearly?' she asked.
My obvious discomfiture seemed to satisfy her. She ignored me for the rest of the evening.

★

The season deepened. What had once been growing canes became large expanses of parched straw as they were chopped down and the trucks and tractors took them away ton by ton.

The overseers walked up and down in their wide straw hats. They were fat, potbellied men with thick books from which they looked up and thundered orders to the men who chopped and the women who heaped the canes together and loaded them onto the waiting trucks.

Sis was one of the few who chopped cane. She did it because the choppers were paid fifty cents more than the loaders. It was very hard work but she had grown accustomed to it.

'Your sister is a chopper coz . . .' Tin Tin seemed reluctant to continue.

'Coz what?'

'Coz she in favour.'

'Ah don' unnerstan'.'

'Chupid boy! She have two overseer boyfren!'

'Don say dat 'bout my sister, Tin. I goin' tell 'er!' I was hurt — deeply hurt. My sudden anger surprised me.

'Favour for favour, my modder say!'

'Don say dat 'bout my sister!' I was close to tears, in a fever; no longer afraid of her.

'Well, is what I hear say.'

Revenge, I thought. She was hurting me because she hadn't done the exams.

'She work same like everybody. Same-same-same!! *Harder* dan your modder an' fadder put togedder!' I couldn't stop pounding my knee. 'Is not ongly man should chop cane fo' money.'

'Okay, Baldie, awright. I didn't mean it. I sorry.'

'I goin' tell 'er, you hear! I goin' tell 'er.'

'Sorry, Baldie, sorry.'

'Don' talk to me.'

We didn't speak for weeks. Tin Tin tried to make up to me several times and finally gave up, which disappointed me greatly since I had planned to soften a bit the next time she came.

I tied out the goats, waited for Sis with her cup of water and studied her with a greater care — a deeper love, I think. I asked her no more questions; barely spoke. I was becoming like her.

I really missed Tin's companionship. Moreso, because the nights of the chill, bright moons had come. We should have been sitting with the rest of the village children on the mounds of cut canes, sucking away and talking about anything that came to mind.

We talked about the world, the things we had heard and read of — strange inventions, planes that flew backwards, machines that talked; wondering about all these and how our world of sugar canes did fit into it all; conscious of, but not questioning the fact that our dreams for ourselves hardly ever went beyond the tallest canes.

Nothing compared with the pleasure we got from invading the fields of growing cane. You would hear the dull *Poks!* as we broke the soft stems, the swish of the swordlike leaves as we hauled the plant — root and all into the road.

There was a watchman stalking somewhere in the night out there, but we didn't care. He never caught anyone. Besides, it didn't feel like stealing. There was something there though, as yet barely perceived, almost vengeful, in this act. We called it breaking cane.

I had passed my exams; had done well enough to go to the secondary school of my choice. My name was even in the papers.

The following week, Tin Tin brought me a sapodilla. It was big, fat and ripe. It smelled so good, I almost fainted. It would be my first for the season. We often did this with our first fruit. We would come together and argue over the first bite. The first fruit was always the best. You got more than just its taste; you got the promise of a whole season of ripeness ahead.

I had suddenly forgotten our quarrel and all the weeks of not speaking to her. I wanted the first bite.

'I wan' de firs' bite.'

'Uh-uh,' she grinned.

'Gimme de firs' bite, nuh.'

'You say, 'nuh'. Dat mean you don' want it.'

'Yeh, man, gimme de sappo, nuh!'

'You say 'nuh' again.'

'Jus' one bite.'

'Okay, come for de bite.' There was a light in her eyes. I was blind to everything else but the fruit. I came forward. She opened her mouth and bit me hard. Tin

Tin couldn't stop laughing. She then offered me the whole fruit. I ate half and offered her the rest. She shook her head.

I had never seen her so serious and easy-to-hurt before. I couldn't deny her a taste of our first sapodilla.

'Don' want mo,' I said. 'I full up.'

'Tek it, I bring it for you.'

She was lying and knew I knew it . There must be a catch, I thought.

'What you want for it?' I asked.

'Nuffing. Lets go an' break cane.'

In a week or two, the season would be over. It was evening; I had already tied the goats in.

We had a favourite spot where we used to retreat to chew our cane and argue. It was the steps of what used to be a plantation house whose former immensity could still be judged by the colossal slabs of stones that made up its now decaying foundation and walls.

'You find ruins like dis all over de country, in all dem islands, always on de highest hill, lookin' down.' I once commented to Sis, pointing at a similar picture in my History book. 'I wonder why nobody never bother to pull dem down or p'raps buil' dem back?'

'Lots o' things remain, besides dem old house,' muttered my sister. 'If I have my way, I pull everyt'ing down, dig up de foundation an' start clean — start new!'

'Talk to me, Baldie,' Tin Tin said.

'Bout what?'

'Anyfing. Like we uses, erm; like we custom.'

'Bout when we get big, you mean?'

'Yup.'

'Okay, like I tell you; we goin buil' a house wid — lemme see — nine room an . . .'

'No, ten — you say ten is a balance' number, member?'

'Oh, yes — ten. And after?' I sought confirmation.

'Don' ask me. *You* tell me.' She was suddenly angry.. 'You ferget arready? You jus' start goin' to Secondary an' you ferget arready! Go ahead.'

'An mebbe, mebbe we married, long as you don' beat

me up when I mek you vex,' I added.

'You never say 'mebbe' before.'

'Well . . .'

'Wish I was a boy an didn' have no lil brother an sister to care for. Then I woudda show you.'

'Is not my fault.'

'Is mines?' she snapped. She paused, then asked: 'What you wan become?'

'Lawyer mebbe; p'raps doctor — make a lot o' money.'

'You don' wan' to drive cane-truck no more?'

'Don fink so. Why you ask me all dem questions, Tin?' Cuz is not fair.'

'Is not my fault.'

'You say dat again, I rap you.'

'Well is . . .' I stopped short. I thought I knew how she felt. I had never seen her so defeated before.

'I hate cane,' I said suddenly, viciously.

'Me too,' Tin Tin whimpered, close to tears. We rose and, together, picked our way over the stones of the same road that I watched the women travelling on every evening after work.

'Baldie,' she said shortly, her voice clear and strong again. 'I hate cane too. Cane not always sweet, you see. It have some dat salt, some dat coarse. It spoil you teeth; an if you not careful, you cut your mout' wit de peelin. Take my fadder: take your fadder. See what happen? Dats why I don' like no sugar in my tea. I 'fraid I might be drinkin im.'

She was talking like my sister. Did they all talk like that when things were not settled in their minds?

'I startin' off on Monday, Tin.' I felt I had to tell her.

'I know.'

We were almost home. She smiled — her first for the day, I guessed.

'Luck, Baldie.' Tin Tin was looking into my face. She meant it.

'I see you tomorrow?' I begged, making a mental note to remember that it was ten rooms, not nine.

'Dunno, Baldie.'

'We goin break cane togedder, right?' I pleaded.

'Don fink so, Baldie,' she answered. She dropped my hand and sprinted off home.

If ever I needed Sis to talk to me, it was this time.

'Sis?'

'Huh?'

'Why Tin Tin tell me good luck as if I done dead o' something? Like if she never goin' see me again? She don' even wan' to talk to me no more. She say if everybody can't get eddicated, den nobody should.'

'Coz she unnerstan'.'

'Unnerstan' what?' I demanded.

Sis looked at me, then, and began to speak so slowly, you could barely see her lips move: 'Coz dem offerin' you a chance — a ticket so's you could up an leave after; leave like you modder, *alone,* and never come back; leave everybody here, behind. Tin Tin shoudda gone before you — you know dat?'

I do not know how to say it, except that her eyes were burning. I mean it. Whenever she spoke like that, they seemed to gather all the lamplight and hold it in — sort of glowing.

It used to frighten me because she was no longer my sister when she became like this. She was somehow bigger and stronger and stranger than anyone I had ever known or dreamed of, staring past me, through the walls, beyond the night. Beyond! . . . I didn't seem to matter as much as the thing she was staring at.

'What you want to become?' She had pushed the new uniform on the table in front of me as though I had only to put it on to become whatever I wanted.

'Tin Tin ask me de same question.'

'An you tell 'er?'

'Yep: doctor mebbe o' lawyer.'

'No!!'

I looked up, surprised. Her eyes were still bright — still staring beyond me.

'We don' need no lawyers now an we been gettin' along fine widdout doctors. We wan teachers and a school firs'!'

'But we talkin 'bout *me;* not no teacher an' no school. Who it have to teach round . . .'

'We,' she hissed. I never knew a person's face could hold so many emotions at the same time.

'Teach, Baldie, coz Secandry ain't no real escape. Long as we tie down you tie down too. It ain't enough fo' you to go alone. Learnin' to escape cane not enough. How to *break* it — break *out* ov it, is what you have to learn. You unnerstan?'

I shook my head; I wasn't sure.

'Tin Tin unnerstan: *Sheez* de real canebreaker!'

'I could break cane too!' I was hating them for making me feel so confused.

'Den teach! Wen de time come, buil' a school an stay right here an teach de children so'z it don' have no mo' Tin Tin; so'z it don' have no mo *me* right? Canebreakers *before* lawyers!'

She was suddenly human again. The light had gone out of her eyes. I felt tired, washed out. I wished she hadn't thrown that weight on me, that she hadn't started me thinking and, for the first time, seeing the deepening lines of fatigue on her face.

I wished I would still experience the pleasure of handing her a cup of water and watching her drink away the day's hardship.

You see, she was pushing me to see things in a big, wide way, like Tin Tin sometimes did. As yet, I barely understood; but for once, my friends, I thought I glimpsed it — what she had been staring at that night, past me and beyond. And believe me, I was almost blinded by it. I looked at her and was shaken; even frightened by the power of such patience; the basis of such anger — so 'erm, no-no! I don' have no regrets about anyfing; 'specially in this resolve I mek to remain.

Awright class there goes the bell. Straighten up now. Before you leave, please make a note of tomorrow's topic. It would help discussion if you read it at home in advance. Page forty-seven to fifty-two — 'Plantation Societies' by P. Jameson. What's that? Yes . . . .

Some Books Published by Karia Press

Available through Bookshops or direct from Karia Press, BCM Karia, London, WC1N 3XX, United Kingdom. Tel: (01) - **249 4446**

For direct orders, enclose payment with order. (Also add handling charge of 15% UK; 20% Overseas)

Short Stories/ Prose Fiction

Song For Simone
and other stories

by Jacob Ross

ISBN 0 946918 29 5 Pb £3.95
ISBN 0 946918 33 3 Hb £8.95

The Day Sharon Lost Her Way Home

by Jennifer Martin
Illustrated by Paul Dash

ISBN 0 946918 23 6 Pb £3.95
ISBN 0 946918 24 4 Hb £5.95

The Earliest Patriots:
Being the true adventures of certain survivors of 'Bussa's Rebellion' (1816), in the island of Barbados and Abroad

by Evelyn O'Callaghan

ISBN 0 946918 53 8 Pb £2.95

Afrikan Lullaby
Folk Tales From Zimbabwe

by Chisiya

ISBN 0 946918 45 7 Pb £1.95

Biography/ Autobiography

The Autobiography of A Zimbabwean Woman

by Sekai Nzenza

ISBN 0 946918 21 X Pb £4.95
ISBN 0 946918 22 8 Hb £8.95

Dispossessed Daughter of Africa

by Carol Trill

ISBN 0 946918 42 2 Pb £4.95
ISBN 0 946918 42 0 Hb £8.95

In Troubled Waters
Memoirs of my Seventy Years in England

by Ernest Marke

ISBN 0 946918 2 5 Pb £4.95

"I Think of My Mother"
Notes on the Life and Times of Claudia Jones

by Buzz Johnson

ISBN 0 946918 02 3 Pb £3.95
ISBN 0 946918 05 8 Hb £8.95

This list represents some books already in print and those soon to be published. For a full list of published and forthcoming publications please write to the address above.

Black People in Britain

We Are Our Own Educators!
Josina Machel: From Supplementary to Black Complementary School

by Valentino A. Jones

ISBN 0 946918 37 6 Pb £3.95

Telling The Truth
The Life and Times of the British Honduran Forestry Unit in Scotland (1941-44)

by Amos Ford

ISBN 0 946918 01 5 Pb £2.95
ISBN 0 946918 03 1 Hb £7.95

Many Struggles
West-Indian Workers and Service Personnel in Britain 1939-45

by Marika Sherwood

ISBN 0 946918 04 X Pb £3.95
ISBN 0 946918 00 7 Hb £8.95

Language

Caribbean & African Languages:
Social History Language, Literature and Education

by Morgan Dalphinis

ISBN 0 946918 06 6 Pb £6.95
ISBN 0 946918 07 4 Hb £16.95

Language and Liberation:
Creole Language Politics in the Caribbean

by Hubert Devonish

ISBN 0 946918 27 9 Pb £5.95
ISBN 0 946918 27 8 Hb £9.95

New Poetry

Because The Dawn Breaks!
Poems Dedicated to the Grenadian People

by Merle Collins
With Introduction by Ngũgĩ Wa Thiong'o

ISBN 0 946918 08 2 Pb £3.95
ISBN 0 946918 09 0 Hb £8.95

For Those Who Will Come After!

by Morgan Dalphinis

ISBN 0 946918 10 4 Pb £3.95
ISBN 0 946918 11 2 Hb £8.95

Word Rhythms From the Life of A Woman

by Elean Thomas

ISBN 0 946918 40 6 Pb £3.95
ISBN 0 946918 41 4 Hb £8.95

Rapso Explosion

by Bro. Resistance

ISBN 0 946918 34 1 Pb £3.95